The Noble Flame

Mary Livingston

Contents

Chapter 1

N orwood, Derbyshire

August, 1813

"Christopher Kensington," Kit murmured to the election official, who subsequently went down his list of landowning men in the district to find his name.

"That is Sir Christopher Kensington, I will have you now," Cassian corrected proudly.

"Father, please," Kit hushed. He was still not at all comfortable with the attention, and the knighthood it had brought. It was all sort of silly, really. He had only been in the right place at the right time.

Kit had been a student at Cambridge University for the last four years. He had completed his studies in June, and had now permanently returned to Derbyshire to help his father run his textile business.

But his last month at Cambridge had been far more eventful than any before that. Prince Edward, the younger son of King William V had been completing his first year of study, just as Kit had been finishing. Kit had been leaving an examination when he noticed an unusual man skulking across the school grounds. He had looked agitated and angry.

Kit had been making his way towards the man to ask him what was the matter when he saw him produce a pistol from the inside of his coat. His target was the young prince, sitting by himself reading.

It had been instinct, really. Kit had cried out to the prince and tackled the would-be assassin to the ground.

Kit had gained much from the ordeal. The King had given him a knighthood and had offered a generous income, not that Kit had accepted. He was famous and was lauded a hero. But Kit was most glad to come away from the situation with a friend.

Of course his parents could not have been prouder. His mother could not stop parading him about and introducing him to everyone as Sir Kit. He would have been annoyed were he not so happy to have parents that wanted to brag about him.

Kit would never take them for granted. Ever.

"Sir Christopher, forgive me," muttered the official. He marked Kit's name, then Cassian's, and then Finn's.

It was the district election between the sitting MP and another candidate. The election was being held in the church as it was the largest room in town. Inside, landowning men from all over had come to cast their votes between the two idiots.

Supporters from both sides were hawking, campaigning for their candidate, waving flyers about trying to sway voters at the last minute.

Kit had no idea who he was going to vote for as he took his ballot over to the station. He had to choose between two names, but both were as corrupt and self-serving as each other. It seemed one had to choose between the lesser of two evils.

The sitting MP, Sir John Strachan, had voted against improving rights for the poor in parliament. Kit supposed that was unforgivable. With a sigh, he dipped his quill in ink and marked the box of the opponent. Kit hoped he would do well should he be lucky enough to be elected.

"How is Faith doing?" asked Finn once all three men had cast their votes and left the church. They stood together on the road. The streets were relatively quiet as most of the village was inside the church.

"She is a nervous wreck," replied Cassian honestly.

Kit could see the anxiety on his father's face.

"Why don't you delay the operation until after she has the baby?" proposed Finn.

"Because Faith won't let me," confessed Cassian. "You know the operation was scheduled before we learned we were to have another child. Doctor Ward is travelling from Leicestershire to remove the bullet and Faith won't see the procedure cancelled."

Kit was nervous, too, but he would not show it. The bullet that lay dormant all these years in his father's chest had long been a source of anxiety for Faith. But it had never been the right time to have it removed.

First they were adjusting to their new life. And then Kit's younger sister, Emma, was born. Kit had gone off to university and so he could not be home to help. And so Faith had finally decided enough was enough, and had written to the Leicestershire doctor herself to arrange a date.

One week later Cassian and Faith learned they were to have another child. But Faith would not change her mind, no matter how worried she was.

"Everything will be fine," promised Finn.

"Oh, I am not worried about myself," Cassian replied. "I am worried about Faith. She is all nerves. I fear what it might do to the child."

Kit did not like to hear that. He just wanted the procedure to be over with. He did not like seeing his mother uneasy, especially in her condition.

"We are expecting you for dinner tonight?" checked Cassian.

"Oh, absolutely. I shall distract Faith by asking to hear the story of Kit's bravery again," Finn said teasingly. "Until then." Just as Finn went to turn away in the direction of the magistrate's office, the doors of the church bust open, and two gruff looking officials were dragging a man out by his upper arms.

Not before descending the steps, they threw him down onto the ground roughly. The force of impact caused the man to smack into the dusty road, his tricorn fell from his head.

The moment it did so, waves of distinctive red hair fell down his back... his?

The woman's back was to Kit, but there was something about that hair, something familiar.

The officials were not finished with her yet. They marched down the church steps with anger in their eyes.

Kit saw it before it happened. One man drew back his foot, ready to kick her in the stomach. Kit saw red, and immediately bellowed, "Stop!"

He did. He put his foot back on the ground as she woman hunched over on all fours, recovering from the fall.

Kit, Cassian and Finn marched over to the altercation.

"You treat a woman like that again, sir, and you will spend the night in a cell," threatened Finn.

Both officials paled. "But sir," the first protested. "She was breaking the law."

"She was voting, sir. We caught her red handed. Impersonating a gentleman. We thought it funny she didn't look eighty years old," added the second.

"Don't I have just as much right as any to decide what idiotic backside represents me in London?" muttered the girl from the ground.

Her voice, too, seemed familiar.

"No, you don't!" retorted the first official. "Woman are too sensitive for such things. It's science. Tell her, sir," he urged Finn.

"What happened to the vote?" asked Finn.

"Caught and destroyed. It did not contaminate the legitimate votes."

"Can you stand, young lady?" Finn pressed his lips together firmly.

Kit had never before seen a woman have the nerve to attempt a vote at an election. He was impressed, just as much as he was saddened that she would have to be dealt with.

She climbed to her feet, brushing the dust off of her breeches. Despite her nerve, she did not disguise herself well. Her figure alone was a dead giveaway. She was far too slim and small to be a man. Kit had not noticed that while she had been on the ground. Her hair, though, was extraordinary.

The moment she turned around, Kit recognised her. His memories immediately took him back to his fourteen year old self, awkwardly following the prettiest girl he had ever seen on her mission to educate her village. He cherished several things about that day, most notably the kiss he had received from her, and his promise to write to her. A promise that he did not keep.

Olivia Pendleton had grown into a stunning young woman. Her face was no longer round and childlike, but elegant and slender. Her skin was like porcelain, with a healthy flush in her cheeks from the summer sun. Her nose was slightly longer, and her lips were fuller than he remembered, but her eyes, just like her hair, were exactly the same. The same brilliant blue, filled with spirit and determination.

"Do you understand what you have done, young lady?" Finn asked seriously.

"I have held my MP accountable for his actions, sir," replied Olivia calmly.

"You have voted in an election illegally," countered Finn.

Kit looked sideways at his father, but he did not see any recognition on Cassian's face. Perhaps he did not know this was Olivia.

Olivia had not looked at Kit, either. She was fixated on Finn, and was standing her ground. She was exactly as Kit remembered her.

"I admire your spirit, Miss ...?"

"Murray," lied Olivia.

Finn saw through it. "Would you like to try again?"

Olivia shook her head. "Take me to prison if you wish it." Olivia held out her wrists, awaiting shackles.

Finn chuckled. "I will handle it from here, gentlemen," Finn dismissed the officials. "Please see me before ejecting any voters violently in future," he added warningly.

The officials retreated back into the church.

"Follow me," instructed Finn. He turned his back on Olivia had started towards the magistrate's office.

Kit could see the frustration on Olivia's face as she obeyed Finn.

Kit and Cassian followed behind. "Your mother is not to hear about this," Cassian said under his breath.

Kit paled. So Cassian had recognised Olivia.

"You know what sort of stress she is under at the moment. If she knew about this, it would put her in a royal state."

Kit nodded, agreeing. Faith could not know about this.

Kit and Cassian followed Finn and Olivia into the magistrate's office. Finn collected his keys from the desk drawer and walked over to the lone cell and unlocked it. Holding the door open, he motioned for Olivia to enter.

Kit could see the ire on Olivia's face as she trudged into the cell. Once inside, she sat down on the small cot as Finn locked the door. Olivia wrapped her arms around her legs and rested her chin on her knees.

"What is going to happen to her?" asked Kit, attempting to mask the fear in his voice. Would Olivia go to prison for this?

"Oh, nothing. I will leave her in there for a few hours to fret. She is just a spirited girl, not a criminal. I will have her parents collect her when she decides to tell me her name."

Kit knew quite a lot about Olivia's parents. Their names were taboo in the Kensington household.

"Her name is Olivia Pendleton," Cassian told Finn. "Her parents are John and Ruth Pendleton. You remember Faith's in-laws."

Realisation dawned on Finn as he turned his head back to Olivia and furrowed his brow. "Oh, yes, I remember," he murmured. "Well, I suppose I shall write to them."

"You can write them but they will not respond!" Olivia shouted from her cell. "I am my Aunt Lorna's problem now."

Kit frowned. Had John and Ruth cast Olivia out? Their only daughter?

Finn pulled a piece of fresh parchment from his desk drawer and scrawled "Lorna" on the page. "Thank you. And where does this Aunt Lorna live?"

Olivia huffed as she confessed. "She and my Grandpapa live on the Murray estate two villages over."

"Did you know about this?" Finn asked Cassian.

Kit did not wait to hear his father's reply. He slipped away towards the cell. Kit came to stand in front of the bars, looking in on Olivia.

Olivia stood up from the cot and came to stand in front of Kit. Her small stature made Kit feel even taller than he already was. She was looking up at him with such conviction in her eyes.

There was so much passion and determination in Olivia. So much spirit. She had been just the same when he had known her seven years earlier. Olivia had purpose.

It was a feeling Kit had yet to experience. What was it like to be so passionate about something that you would break the law for it?

Olivia cocked her head and appeared puzzled. "Why do you stare at me so, stranger?" Olivia asked curiously.

"Stranger?" repeated Kit. Oh, good Lord. She did not even remember him.

Chapter 2

Olivia immediately cracked, a wide smile spreading across her face and a humorous laugh escaping her mouth. She placed her hands on the bars of her cell and pressed her face in between the gap while looking up at him.

"You are Kit Kensington. You boasted of your strength to me before promptly falling on your backside when trying to move my crate of books. You were an orphan before your father found you and you learned to read later in your life and were embarrassed by it. You find me odd, but you did call me extraordinary. I shall never forget that."

Olivia spoke in a hushed tone so that their company would not hear them. She stared at him, not breaking eye contact. Olivia had not forgotten a thing from their brief encounter. But had she recalled their ki –

"I even remember the exact shade of pink your cheeks turn when you are kissed," she added deviously.

Much to Kit's humiliation, his cheeks were undoubtedly rosy. "Alright, you remember," he murmured.

As a fourteen year old boy, Kit had had little to do with the opposite sex. Yes, there had been girls in the care of the reverend, but he had never conversed with a girl his own age, and he certainly had never been enchanted by a girl before, much less a girl like Olivia.

Olivia was rare. She had been extraordinary to him then, and she was still extraordinary to him now. Kit did not quite understand her, but it made him all the more curious.

"It is good to see you again, Olivia," Kit said, extending his hand through the bars of the cell. He remembered things, too.

Olivia smiled and shook his hand firmly.

"Like the men do it. A shake, respect. No spit transferring on to hands," he quoted. It had been odd, but Kit enjoyed Olivia's subtle rebelliousness. Clearly, she had grown less subtle.

Olivia smiled. "Exactly right."

Kit knew that he needed to apologise for breaking his promise to write her. He needed to explain. "Miss Pendleton," he addressed her formally, "or Lady?" he corrected. "You are the daughter of an earl, are you not?"

Olivia pursed her lips. "My father might disagree with you on that subject." She shook her head. "You may call me Olivia and I will call you Kit, just as we were," she decided.

"Olivia," began Kit, "I need to apologise to you for not keeping my promise. I never wrote you and I am sorry."

Olivia's face softened. "You did not injure me, Kit," she told him. "I assure you, it takes a lot more than a broken promise to injure me."

Kit believed her. Here she stood, in a prison cell, with a smile on her face and determination in her heart. Olivia would not be dissuaded nor would she be discouraged by such things as empty words.

"Sometimes it is healthy to be a little selfish. Clearly, others needed you more."

Kit looked back over his shoulder at his father. Cassian was sitting beside Finn, drinking something amber coloured, and chatting quietly. Finn was no longer writing. Perhaps he had ducked out to send the missive to Olivia's aunt without Kit noticing.

Kit had made a promise to himself, and to his family, many years ago, that he would do whatever he needed to in order to make his family happy.

Kit had kept that promise. He had gone to university, just as he was asked to, and he had returned home to help his father run the textile business. He looked after his sisters and helped his mother with her school and protected her however he could.

And now, when he returned home, he would keep his meeting with Olivia Pendleton a secret to keep his mother calm.

Kit did not think he had been selfish a day in his life. Certainly not since he had been a Kensington. He had always done whatever he could to make his family happy, and proud of him. Olivia, on the other hand ...

"Why are you here, Olivia?" Kit asked her, suddenly serious.

Olivia stood firmly, and did not recoil. "Good question," she replied. "I did nothing wrong."

"You broke the law," Kit said dryly.

Olivia's eyes narrowed. "Laws that exist to disadvantage people purely because they do not have a set of bollocks between their legs should not exist," she said icily.

Kit had never before heard such language from a woman's mouth. He grinned, enjoying it. "You are not exempt from the law because you do not agree with it, Olivia," he reminded her.

"I know," she sighed. "Sir John Strachan voted against bills on the improvement of housing, sewerage, the price of grain, the list goes on! All the while lining his own pockets. He governs me just as much as any man. Why do I not have the right to hold him accountable?" Olivia asked Kit seriously.

Olivia was talking of sewerage with an amount of conviction in her voice that Kit had never had. It unsettled him. Where had Olivia's passions come from? And why did Kit not have any of his own?

"I am sorry, I am lecturing you," Olivia apologised. She sunk to her knees and then sat down on the wooden floor. "I have a horrid habit of preaching to others about the things I believe in. I can be quite tiresome."

Kit followed her to the ground. "Never apologise for being passionate, Olivia," Kit said sincerely. "What must it be like to believe in something so whole-heartedly that you would be willing to risk your freedom for it?"

Olivia leaned her head against the bars, a tendril of her long, red hair passing between them temptingly. "Confining," she replied jokingly.

Kit laughed.

"Lonely," Olivia then said softly, her eyes darting nervously to his. "Your parents?"

Olivia shook her head. "My mother and I always had a tumultuous relationship. She never understood me. Nobody ever has, really. I was not the sort of daughter she wanted. I was apprehended when I was sixteen years old for attending a university lecture. I was wearing something similar to this." Olivia gestured to her clothes. "It must not be very convincing," she commented. "My parents settled with the magistrate and I was sent to my Grandpapa Bernard and my Aunt Lorna."

Olivia did not speak with much emotion, but Kit could tell that her mother's rejection had hurt her. Olivia's eyes were quite easy to read.

"Are they good to you?"

Olivia smiled. "Oh, yes." She nodded. "My Grandpapa is a dear. He is eighty years old and quite deaf. He does not know of what I get up to. My Aunt Lorna is my mother's younger sister. She looks after Grandpapa, and she tries to care for me. I am not an easy ward, as you would have gathered. She will be receiving a note any minute informing her of her niece's imprisonment."

"You are not at all changed in these years past," replied Kit. "I am sure your aunt will not be surprised."

Olivia feigned offense. "I am not at all changed? I will have you know I am at least three inches taller," she teased. "You have changed, though," she observed. "You look..."

What? Handsome? Debonair? Charming? Amiable?

"... actually, you look exactly the same," Olivia decided. "You are taller, if that is even possible, and you have grown into your limbs and features, but you look just as cautious as you once did."

"Cautious?" Kit frowned.

"As though you consistently walk through life on eggshells, eager to please and terrified of disappointing," replied Olivia simply.

Kit recoiled. "I am not eager to please, and I certainly am not terrified of disappointing people." Kit could not believe that Olivia had made such an assumption of his character. She had known him for a collective ninety minutes, if that. She knew nothing about him.

"Perhaps I am wrong then." Olivia shrugged her shoulders and moved away from the cell bars. "You ought to stop talking to me. I do not think your father approves and I should hate for you to displease him."

Kit shot her an angry glare. "You are the one in prison."

"Am I?" she countered.

Kit hissed as he climbed to his feet and marched across the room to re-join his father and Finn. He sat down in the spare chair and huffed angrily.

"Are you alright?" asked Cassian, concerned. "What did she say to you?"

"She is not as clever as she thinks she is," Kit mumbled angrily.

"There you are, Cassian. No attachment, whatsoever. Nothing to worry about," Finn said, pleased.

"What?" asked Kit.

Cassian placed a hand on Kit's shoulder. "I was worried that you were becoming quite enamoured with Olivia for a moment," he admitted. "You, of course, understand why such an attachment could never continue. But my worry was for nought. You were always a good boy, Kit. You always do what is right for our family. Once Olivia's aunt comes to collect her, we can put this behind us."

While his father's words were kind, they annoyed him. Kit shoved Olivia's assumptions aside and attempted to smile. There was nothing wrong with pleasing people.

"You, young man, need a good girl," said Finn. "Someone kind and caring, and lacking the criminal urge." He smirked.

"So do you," countered Cassian.

Finn's bachelor status was a constant topic of conversation. He was four and thirty years old and had not married, nor courted, in all the years that Kit had known him.

"At this point, if a pretty woman walked through that door and said that she wanted me, I would drop down on one knee immediately," replied Finn.

As if fate were listening, the door to the magistrate's office flew open, and a young, attractive, red-headed woman burst through the door. She held Finn's note in her right hand.

"Where is the magistrate?" she demanded to know. "I want him!"

Finn stared at her in awe as Cassian burst out laughing. "Go on then!" he urged. "Propose!"

The woman looked confused and utterly unamused. There was no question of the relation. This woman was Olivia's Aunt Lorna. Her hair was much the same shade of red as Olivia's, but she wore it in a braid atop her head, a few strands falling loose from the journey. Her skin had the same porcelain appearance as Olivia's, and her face was just as elegant and feminine. The only difference was that Lorna's eyes were brown, and she looked only a few years older.

Finn cleared his throat as he stood up. Cassian and Kit followed suit. "My name is Finnegan Kelly, ma'am. I am the magistrate."

Lorna huffed. "Lorna Murray," she replied. "Where is Olivia?"

"I am here, Aunt Lorna," Olivia called from her cell.

Lorna's head turned towards Olivia's voice, before her attention returned to Finn. "Mr Kelly, what is this I hear of you arresting my niece for voting?"

"Your hearing is perfectly fine. I did arrest your niece for voting."

Lorna did not at all look like she was in the mood for humour. Her brown eyes narrowed as she approached Finn's desk. She kept eye contact with Finn. Olivia had indeed inherited her courage. "I want her released this minute. My father would be terribly distressed if he learned of this." Lorna's words did not sound at all like emotional blackmail, but genuine worry for her father. Perhaps he was unwell, as well as almost deaf.

Finn had said that he would release Olivia in a few hours. He knew she was not a criminal. "Well, what is in it for me if I release her?" Finn was going to vex her, just as he did Faith quite frequently.

Lorna's eyes flared. "Are you asking for a bribe?" she asked, disgusted.

"Of sorts." Finn grinned. "What is your niece's release worth to you?"

Cassian and Kit exchanged a glance. Clearly Finn had immediately taken a fancy to Lorna and was doing his best to make her as flustered as possible.

Lorna folded her arms across her chest. "What do you want?"

"Just a kiss, right here." Finn tapped his cheek.

Lorna's cheeks nearly turned as crimson as her hair. "You are a pig," she hissed.

"A pig with the keys to your niece's cell," Finn teased.

Lorna balled her hands into fists and stomped around the desk to stand next to Finn. "You promise she will be released? I have your word?"

"My word as a gentleman," promised Finn.

"Something I would believe if you were one," snapped Lorna.

"Oh," feigned Finn. "You wound me, Miss Murray."

"Hush."

Kit could see what Finn was going to do before he did it. Just as Lorna stood up on her toes to kiss Finn's cheek, Finn turned his head and caught her lips. Lorna pulled away immediately in shock, and brought her hand up to smack his cheek. The sound was mighty, and Finn staggered away laughing.

Lorna seized Finn's set of keys from his desk and stormed over to Olivia's cell to unlock it. As soon as the door was open, Lorna grabbed Olivia's hand and pulled her towards the door. Lorna's cheeks were still incredibly flushed, and she dared not look up at the three men in the room.

Olivia, on the other hand, was very amused. "Until we meet again, Kit," she said in farewell as her aunt dragged her out of the magistrate's office and away from view.

"You are cruel," scolded Cassian, amused.

"Ah, yes, but now I get to grovel. I find that women enjoy it when men grovel," replied Finn as he sat back down in his chair. "She was very lovely, though, wasn't she?"

"I choose not to answer that." Cassian grinned and motioned for Kit to follow him as he went to leave the office. "We had best take our leave. Faith will expect you promptly at seven o'clock for dinner."

Finn waved them off as Cassian and Kit walked out onto the street.

Olivia and Lorna were nowhere to be seen. They must have left in a carriage.

"Not a word to your mother," reminded Cassian. "And promise me you will not go seeking that girl out. Nothing good can come from bringing any one of the Pendletons back into Faith's life."

Olivia's observations had angered him. He was still angered by them. But he could not deny that there was truth to them. He endeavoured to please his family. He would do anything to make them happy, even at the expense of his own wants.

Kit knew that he would move past his anger towards Olivia, and quickly, and when he did, he would want to see her again. What his family did not know could not hurt them, he supposed.

Chapter 3

"Remember, not a word to Faith about seeing Olivia," Cassian reminded Kit. "I will speak to Finn at dinner this evening. Something tells me he will want to see Miss Murray again."

Kit would comply. But what was Cassian planning to do should Finn and Miss Murray begin courting? Would not Faith notice a familiar looking red-headed woman at the dinner table?

"There you both are!" cried Faith the minute Kit and Cassian stepped inside Norwood Cottage.

Faith moved quickly down the stairs to meet them in the foyer. Faith appeared very hot and bothered. She wore a light, pale green dress to cope with the August heat. Though her cheeks were still flushed and her dark, curly hair was falling out of her bun.

"I have prepared a bedroom for Doctor Ward," Faith told Cassian. "Well, the servants did. Mr Wade refuses to let me do a thing in my condition." She looked down at the small protrusion between her hips.

The village doctor estimated that Faith was about four months along in her pregnancy. Kit was certain his mother would be excited about it when Cassian's surgery was over and done with and she never needed to fret about lead poisoning again.

Cassian put an arm around Faith and kissed her temple. Faith visibly relaxed. Cassian then began to lead her towards the drawing room. Before they were gone, Faith looked over her shoulder. "Oh, Kit," she called, "you have a visitor in the library." She smiled at him.

A visitor? Kit had not been expecting anyone. Kit's mind immediately took him to Olivia, totally unwillingly. He did not like the swell of hope he felt in his stomach. It was foreign and unsettling. His fond memories of Olivia did not outweigh the anger he still felt towards her.

Kit made his way down the hallway to the library. Just as soon as he put his hand on the doorhandle, he had a thought. Faith would not be fretting about a doctor's accommodation if a Pendleton was in her house.

Kit pushed open the door to see a familiar face in a rather odd setting.

There were four people in the library. Kit's two younger sisters, Lucy's little friend, Violet Barry, and His Royal Highness, Prince Edward.

Lucy and Violet were sitting together on an armchair, a fairy tale book between them. Emma sat up at the desk with Edward with her china tea set she had been gifted last Christmas.

Emma was pouring imaginary tea for a prince. Were it not so embarrassing Kit would laugh.

"Your Royal Highness," remarked Kit in disbelief.

Kit's time at Cambridge had been relatively quiet. He had attended his classes and completed his tasks. He took full advantage of the education his father wanted for him. Of course, when news got around that the King's younger son would be attending the university, there was rather a lot of excitement.

Kit hardly saw him. The prince was three years younger than he was, and so they shared no common lectures; not that the prince was very studious. In fact, the assassination attempt had occurred on one of the few days Prince Edward had actually been present on school grounds.

Kit was still unused to his official title. It seemed strange that a once unwanted orphan was a knight. Either way, Kit would have been content with the prince's friendship.

Kit and Edward had become friends over the course of the summer. Kit had been summoned to London at the beginning of July, and he and Cassian had learned that Kit was being awarded a knighthood for his bravery by the King. Since then, he and Edward had been in frequent company.

Edward had more recreational time, or so he claimed. He had perfect elder siblings to see to the royal duties.

"I am incognito," replied Edward humorously. He gestured to his plain clothing. "It is just a little too hot for me at the minute, Miss Emma. Do you mind if I drink it in a little while?" Edward spoke to six year old Emma tenderly.

Emma nodded, her dark curls bouncing.

"Is that why my sister is serving you tea and not our butler?"

Edward grinned and joined Kit at the library door. "I prefer the imaginary kind anyway."

"What are you doing here?" asked Kit. "I thought you were going back to Cambridge for the beginning of term?"

Edward grinned sheepishly. "I have decided not to go back to Cambridge this year."

Kit frowned and closed his eyes. Perhaps it was because she was on his mind, but he was immediately reminded of something Olivia had once told him.

"Education is a right, and not a privilege. Or at least it will be if I have anything to do with it."

Kit opened his eyes. Taking his father's pocket watch from his waist coat, he checked the time. "Lucy, it is nearly five o'clock. Violet ought to be going along home now."

Both girls jumped off of the arm chair and returned the book to its shelf, before quickly heading towards the library door.

"I do wish you could come to play at my house, Lucy," Violet said forlornly as she covered her blonde braids with a pink bonnet. "I do not understand why Mama will not let you."

Lucy grimaced as she showed her friend the door. She changed the subject away from her sore spot. Lucy was well aware of why she was not allowed to play at Violet's house. She was not stupid; she heard what people said about her. "Let us go and find Mr Wade so he can fetch your carriage." The two girls left the library.

"Why is she not allowed to play at her friend's house? Is she really so poorly behaved?"

Edward was clearly trying to distract him. "No, she is an angel. Mrs Barry is just a prejudiced old bat," Kit snapped. "Emma, can you please go and feed Cat?"

Emma scooted down off of the chair excitedly, calling for their dog, Cat.

"I did not know you have a cat," remarked Edward.

"He's a dog," replied Kit. "But that is not what we need to discuss. Why would you give up your studies?"

Edward sighed exasperatedly. "What exactly must I study for? I am not going to be king. Charles is. He is the good son."

Kit could not pretend to be privy to the inner relations of the royal family, but it was clear that Edward and his father did not have the most loving relationship. Edward's elder brother, Charles, was clearly the preferred son. Charles was being groomed to be king. Edward's elder sister, Alice, like Charles, was also adored by her father, and the country, too. Alice was very diplomatic and level-headed, and was one of the few the king trusted for advice, which was why she had not been married off yet.

"Education should be a right, and not a privilege, but it is not. Unfortunately, that is not how the world works. Those who have the means have the opportunity to better themselves. You have an opportunity, sir!"

"Call me Edward, for goodness' sake. You are three years my senior," Edward muttered. "Someone else can have my place. And I did not come here to be lectured or criticised. If I had wanted that I would have endured an evening with my father."

"You have an opportunity to better yourself."

"To do what?" challenged Edward. "I do not know what I am meant to do, Kit. I know I certainly will not find out by completing a degree in something I am not passionate about. We cannot all be perfect sons like you. Has completing your studies helped you to learn what you are meant for?"

A perfect son?

Kit had attended university because it was an opportunity afforded to him by his father. Cassian wanted Kit to receive the very best education, and Kit was immensely grateful. Only eight years earlier he could not even write his own name.

Kit had studied business because Cassian had wanted him to. Kit had returned home to Derbyshire because he was going to help his father run the textile business.

That had been the plan. It had always been the plan. Nothing else was ever discussed. Cassian and Kit would run the business together. Of course Kit would comply. He always agreed to whatever his parents wanted for him.

Kit was the perfect son. "Olivia was right."

Eggshells, Olivia had called it. She had accused him of walking through life on eggshells, eager to please, and terrified to disappoint.

Olivia was absolutely correct. Kit had a feeling that Olivia was frequently correct about things. Kit walked on eggshells around his family. Whatever they wanted, he would go above and beyond to exceed their expectations. He loved them so much that he so feared their disapproval.

But what was Kit meant for? What was he supposed to do with his life? What were his passions? What were his ambitions? What would make him happy?

"Who is Olivia?" asked Edward.

Kit's train of thought stopped and his attention returned to his friend. Had he said her name out loud? "Olivia ... well, she was arrested today for attempting to vote in the election," Kit said bluntly.

Edward smirked. "Parliament would have conniptions if they knew."

Kit grinned, knowing he was right. But Olivia probably had more brains in her temple than half the men voting today had in their whole heads. "But it is exactly her character. Even when I knew her when she was a girl, she did exactly as she wanted. She followed her passions, and fought for what she believed in, no matter the consequence."

"You knew her?"

"I did," Kit confirmed. "I still know her, and I was terribly rude to her today. I was angry at her, but it turns out she was only observing what I already knew." In her own blunt way, Olivia was only trying to help him.

"I am rude to Alice all the time and she always forgives me. I would not fret. The fairer sex are well aware of the faults of men."

"Do you fancy going out for a ride?" Kit proposed, recalling the address Olivia had given to Finn in order to write to her aunt. Kit had not done one rebellious act in all the years he had been a Kensington. He was about to start.

Chapter 4

O livia sat quietly in the carriage and fiddled with the cuff of the men's shirt she was wearing. It really was quite a comfortable garment, despite being quite the wrong fit. The breeches, too, were quite practical. She supposed, though, that she would have to abide by some of society's rules. It would be back to dresses tomorrow.

What had she done today? Olivia had stolen some of her grandfather's older, smaller garments and has masqueraded as a man at the county election. She had been caught, as she had expected to be.

What had she achieved today? Olivia hoped her actions would start conversation. Elected MP's were just as answerable to their female constituents as they were to the men.

But not so deep down inside, Olivia knew that they all thought she was ridiculous. A silly, rich girl with nothing better to do than throw a tantrum and break the rules without fear of consequence. Rich parents ensured that girls like her would never face a court of law.

Olivia could not ever remember not feeling strongly for the oppressed or the disadvantaged. It was in her nature to help where she could. It was customary for rich families to take a basket of food now and again to poor families, but it never seemed like enough to Olivia.

Olivia grew up with parents who resented her for her sex. They later resented her for much more, but it had started with her gender. Before Olivia could understand land laws and titles, she often wondered what was so wrong with being a girl.

And so she had come across the book: Declaration of the Rights of Woman and of the Female Citizen. Not so much stumbled across as hunted for literature referencing the benefits of being a girl. Instead of finding benefits, Olivia truly came to understand that in this world, women were secondary, inferior to their male counterparts. It was a disadvantage to be female.

Perhaps it was Olivia's natural stubborn character, but she would not simply carry on in such a way. She endeavoured to help those around her. She used funds from her own dowry to fund a teacher's salary for the village children. She donated her father's books, albeit without his permission, to ensure that those people had equal opportunity as adults to provide for themselves and for their families.

As Olivia grew older, her dissatisfaction with what was expected of her grew. Her mother, Ruth, often detested Olivia's "charity" as she called it, and instead forced ladylike lessons on her repeatedly.

Olivia was proficient in the pianoforte, but how would that help anyone? Olivia wanted to see a society in which being a girl was not a disadvantage. She wanted to see woman as celebrated scholars and intellectuals, and God allowing, elected officials. She wanted to see a world in which every person, man or woman, could seek an education, no matter their social standing. She wanted to see people sitting in parliament based on their talents, morals and ideals, and not their social ambitions.

Olivia wanted to change the world. But clearly, she was so very far from doing so.

"Gaol, Olivia," hissed her aunt Lorna. "I wish I could say that this was the first, and last, time that I would be collecting you from a cell, Olivia, but we both know it is not true."

Olivia's parents, Ruth and John, had grown quickly sick of Olivia's "rebellious, ungodly ways". A clergyman for a father always meant Olivia was in for a sound lecture.

At sixteen, after distributing pamphlets promoting the establishment of a women's university in London, Olivia had been arrested for sedition. And, of course, all pamphlets were confiscated and destroyed. Olivia had gone one further and had attended a university lecture, dressed once again as a man. It had resulted in arrest, of course.

Her parents settled with the magistrate for surely some obscene amount. Not for Olivia's benefit, but to preserve their own social image. Ruth had had enough then. Olivia's belongings were tossed into a carriage and she was sent to Derbyshire to live with her maternal grandfather, Bernard Murray, and Ruth's younger half-sister, Lorna.

No matter how strong and stubborn Olivia was, that day, three and a half years ago, would remain as one of the worst days of her life. One did not simply move past being rejected by their parents. It was a heavy burden she still carried.

But coming to live with her grandfather and aunt had been positive. She had known a familial love at Murray Park, her grandfather's estate. Aunt Lorna was more of an older sister to Olivia, as she was only eight years her senior. Lorna attempted to guide Olivia, which was not always an easy task, and she consoled her in her failures, which were many.

Olivia could not understand why her mother had always hated Lorna. She was lovely, even-tempered, kind, and just about the most patient woman in the world.

Well, most of the time. Magistrate's offices were not always her favourite places to visit.

"I am sorry," murmured Olivia.

"Do not lie, dear. We both know you are not sorry," retorted Lorna.

"No, I suppose I am not," admitted Olivia.

Lorna sighed. "One of these days, Olivia, you are not going to walk away consequence-free. You are going to get into real trouble."

The way Olivia saw it, she had two paths she could take in her life. The first, her mother's preference, was the path of a doting, subservient wife and mother. She would marry well, of course; Ruth would see to that. Her husband would be the centre of her world. She would do all she could to raise his standing. She would live comfortably, and have more servants than necessary. Nannies would care for her children, and she would spend her days paying calls to other ladies who were living the same, dull life.

Olivia would suffocate. That life would poison her.

And so her only other option was the second path. She had to fight for the life she wanted. Olivia wanted to be educated and independent. She wanted to have an opinion on things other than parasols, and she wanted to have that opinion heard. If she married, which was highly unlikely, it would be for her own happiness, and to someone who supported her ambitions, and she would do the same in return.

If a man could love her exactly as she was, she could love him forever.

"I am not afraid of punishment, Aunt Lorna," replied Olivia. Prison was preferable to Path One.

"Perhaps we ought to take an excursion to a real prison and you can say that sentence again," mused Lorna. She sighed. "But I know there is not changing your mind. You are like your mother in that way."

Ruth and Olivia were so alike, and yet so different. Each could argue until they were blue in the face, fighting for polar opposite sides.

"Look at you!" Lorna seized one of Olivia's hand, which was grazed.

Olivia enjoyed the maternal concern, and she smiled slightly. "I was thrown out of the church. Landed on my hands."

Lorna rubbed her hand. "Oh, Olivia, what are we going to do with you?"

"Put up with me, I hope."

Lorna chuckled. "Did you know those gentlemen back at the magistrate's office? I heard you refer to the young man by his Christian name. You must be very familiar with him." Her tone was curious, and yet disapproving.

Olivia scoffed. "Oh, Aunt, please. I abhor the suggestion. You were the one who kissed a magistrate to grant my release."

Lorna's cheeks nearly went as red as her hair. "Any word of this to my father and I will have you sleeping with the pigs," she muttered.

"Dear Grandpapa would not hear it anyway," stirred Olivia. Her grandfather was quite nearly deaf. "But yes, you are right, I did know one of them. Two of them." Olivia thought back to that rather frightening day when she was eleven, on the green of her once Uncle George's house. She recalled seeing the magistrate there, too. "All of them, actually."

"How?" Lorna pried.

"Do you remember my Aunt Anne?" asked Olivia. "She was married to my Uncle George. She prefers to be called Faith, now, I think."

"Oh, yes, I remember Anne. I met her once, years ago, at her wedding breakfast. Then, of course, we all saw the papers."

Anne, or Faith's, return from the dead had been well publicised. It was at least a year before the newspapers were free from some mention of the story. It was quite fantastic. A woman returned from the dead with an illegitimate child. A duel. The death of her husband. A marriage to the victor.

"The man with the dark hair, the magistrate's friend, his name is Cassian Kensington," explained Olivia.

Realisation filled Lorna's face as her knowledge of the story filled in the blanks.

"The young man, Kit, is Mr Kensington's son," Olivia continued.

"Mr Kensington looks too young to have a son quite Kit's age," remarked Lorna.

"Kit is Mr Kensington's adopted son," clarified Olivia. "I first met him when I was eleven." Olivia had to look away so that her aunt would not see her blush. She remembered every single second of their first meeting. One did not forget something as pivotal as their first kiss.

Olivia had always had a lot of nerve, but she had still been nervous when she impulsively kissed Kit. She had thought he was very nice looking, with kind features, even if he was very tall and gangly looking. But she had liked him because he had listened, understood, and agreed with her mission at the time.

She had never met anyone who thought her ambition to change the world was not foolish.

Kit was quite changed in his features, now. He had grown into his limbs. He looked like a normal, albeit very tall, young man. His hair was blond, and had a lovely curl to it, and his green eyes were kind. Olivia thought him a very good looking man indeed.

Kit looked well. He looked healthy, and he was dressed very fine indeed. He looked like a gentleman, one who had risen in rank through education. Olivia had wished that for him.

But the way he followed his father troubled her. She had noticed it almost immediately. Kit followed Cassian in a way that did not seem normal to her. Not that she had much experience in obeying her parents, but the way Kit carried himself around his father seemed very odd to her.

Cautious, she had called him, and she had hit a nerve. Olivia very often put her foot in it and caused offense. She had not meant to hurt his feelings, and she felt very bad for it, but instead of apologising, she had only jeered him.

Olivia knew she was right, but she had not meant to hurt Kit. For the briefest of moments, Kit had been one of the only friends she had ever known.

Kit had wondered aloud to her what it would be like to believe in something so whole-heartedly that one would risk their freedom for it. Olivia believed in fighting for the disadvantaged, and promoting the rights of women, and Kit was right, she was willing to risk her freedom for it. Kit surely could not find his passion in complying with what his father wanted.

Olivia was certain Cassian would forbid Kit from ever seeing her again, which made Olivia certain that Kit would obey, but she did hope that she would have the opportunity to apologise. Not only would Cassian consider her a bad influence, but she was also an undesirable relation. She had only been eleven at the time, but she was well aware of hatred towards the Pendletons.

That had been Olivia's first taste of familial rejection. At least it was because of her surname, and not her character.

"Well, I suppose we are lucky you knew them. Mr Kelly was very lenient."

"I have you to thank for that, Aunt," teased Olivia. "I think Mr Kelly liked you."

"Do shut up, Olivia," hushed Lorna bashfully. "Oh, we are home, thank goodness for that."

Murray Park was a dignified country manor that sat situated on a leafy green. There was an abundance of trees on the estate, which made it quite secluded. It was the privacy her grandfather enjoyed.

Olivia and Lorna were greeted by a footman who opened the door for them and lowered the steps. Once inside, they climbed the grand staircase immediately, knowing at this time of evening, Sir Bernard Murray would be enjoying his pipe in his sitting room by the fire.

Sure enough, when they opened the door, Bernard was sitting in his chair, puffing away.

Bernard Murray was a kindly, old gentleman. Descended from Scottish nobility, Bernard was a baronet, and had made his fortune in farming, and lived comfortably, cared for by his favourite daughter, Lorna.

He had been married twice. First, to Olivia's maternal grandmother, Ruth's mother. From what Olivia understood, it had been a very unhappy union, and typhus had taken her before Ruth was out of the nursery. But when Ruth was sixteen, Bernard had married again, and had two further children. A son, Colin, who had married a few years ago and moved to Surrey with his family, and his beloved Lorna.

The marriage had been very happy, and when Mrs Jane Murray had died some five years ago, it about broke Bernard's heart. Lorna had promised never to leave him from then on, and was quite devoted to her father.

Lorna was seven and twenty, and Olivia knew that she would never marry while Bernard was still alive.

Lorna went over to her father, and kissed him on his balding head.

Bernard put down his pipe and beamed at his daughter. "Oh, you are returned, dear Lorna. I wondered where you had got to."

"I did tell you, Papa," replied Lorna, knowing Bernard would not have heard her.

Olivia joined Lorna at her side and smile at her grandfather. Bernard was a sweet looking, very old man. His blue eyes were kind, and had seen many, many years. His once red hair was now white, and his skin was crinkled. Olivia's favourites were the lines around his mouth, achieved through years of smiling.

"Ah, Olivia," he greeted cheerfully, before frowning and inspecting her attire through his spectacles on the end of his nose. "I will never understand the fashions these days."

Olivia gestured to her breeches playfully. "Oh, all the girls are wearing this in London, Grandpapa."

"Did you have a lovely day out, Olivia?" asked Bernard.

"Oh, yes, Grandpapa. I voted in the election, was arrested, and spent a few hours in a cell," Olivia chirped. Lorna rolled her eyes.

"Wonderful, wonderful," replied Bernard as he resumed puffing his pipe.

"Go and have something to eat, Olivia. I am not sure they fed you on your lovely day out." Lorna sat down in the chair opposite her father and picked up the book she had most likely discarded to go and collect Olivia.

Olivia kissed her grandfather and left the sitting room. In doing so, she nearly collided with their butler, Stoughton.

"Oh, pardon me, milady," he excused himself, standing back and straightening his posture. "There are two gentlemen visitors to see you, milady."

Olivia frowned. Two gentlemen? Oh! Perhaps it was Mr Kelly come to arrest her again. Perhaps she was in more trouble than she had originally thought. Oh, dear. It was so easy to dismiss consequences when they never happened. This was actually quite a daunting turn of events.

"Who?" she asked fearfully.

"A Mr Kensington and a Mr Smith, milady," replied Stoughton. "Shall I fetch Miss Murray to chaperone?"

Cassian! What could he want? And who was this Mr Smith? A solicitor? Another magistrate?

"No," she replied quickly. She did not want Lorna witnessing this. "Where are they?"

"I put them in the drawing room, milady."

"Thank you." She dismissed Stoughton and took a deep breath. Whatever this concerned, she knew she had to accept it. Fighting for what she believed in was worth any consequence.

Chapter 5

Stoughton had arrived at the drawing room before her, and announced Olivia's arrival. "Lady Olivia Pendleton."

Olivia passed over the threshold expecting to see Cassian, but instead she was greeted by Kit and a guest she did not recognise.

Both men stood when she entered the room and they bowed their heads respectfully. Truthfully, she had not expected to see Kit ever again, let along receive such courtesy from him.

Olivia went to nervously smooth her skirt, but stopped herself foolishly when she realised she was still wearing a pair of ill-fitting men's breeches and a white shirt.

"Good evening, Olivia," greeted Kit awkwardly. "Please, allow me to introduce my friend, Hi –"

"Mr Smith," interjected his friend. "Edward Smith, milady."

Olivia pursed her lips. That was strange. Nevertheless, she extended her hand in greeting. Kit's friend looked rather dashing, albeit slightly anxious. There was a distinct line between his brows that told her so. His clothes were not as fine as Kit's, so Olivia presumed he might have been a school friend. Regardless, he did have a kind pair of blue eyes that she appreciated. Edward approached her and took her hand in his. Just as he leant down to kiss it, Olivia pulled her hand away.

Edward was taken aback.

"Shake her hand, Edward, like a peer," advised Kit, offering Olivia a reassuring smile.

In receipt of such an affirmation from a gentleman, Olivia felt an unfamiliar flutter of nerves in her stomach. Peer. Perhaps that was her new favourite word. A gentleman had just referred to her as an equal. Olivia thought she might cry. But she could not attribute the nerves to the affirmation. She had smarts enough to owe them to the gentleman who offered the affirmation with a charming smile.

"Forgive me, milady," apologised Edward, a curious smile spreading across his handsome face. He shook her hand firmly, just as he would another gentleman. The anxiety seemed to disappear from Edward's face, and she saw a hint of mischief.

"Not at all, Mr Smith," replied Olivia. "It is a pleasure to make your acquaintance."

"Trust me, the pleasure is all mine." Edward grinned, and Olivia sensed the wicked double entendre. Yes, he was definitely mischievous.

"Alright, that is enough," Kit snapped, dragging Edward away from Olivia. "Olivia, I apologise. You may find Edward a little ... entitled. He is used to getting what he wants."

Olivia gaged that. Nevertheless, she shook her head and offered Kit and Edward a seat. They walked over to the settees, Kit and Edward taking the sofa opposite Olivia. "I am honestly surprised to see you here, Kit," remarked Olivia. "I was sure I had offended you enough to sustain us for another decade of separation."

"That you did," agreed Kit.

"I am sorry for it," Olivia apologised sincerely. "I have a habit of acting and speaking before I think."

"Oh, I noticed."

Olivia felt her cheeks warm. The problem with pale skin was that it betrayed her when she was embarrassed. Her cheeks became nearly as crimson as her hair. She did not dare look up at either gentleman for fear of further embarrassment.

"I did not come here to seek your apology, Olivia. I came here to offer mine."

Olivia forgot her embarrassment and looked up at Kit immediately with a frown. "What?" she asked, confused.

Kit shook his head helplessly. "It took me a little while to realise, but you were right." He sighed. "You were right about everything. I was just too blind to see it."

Olivia had not been expecting that. She forgot her ladylike posture and slouched a little into the settee as she listened.

"I have been walking on eggshells since the day I became a Kensington. I suppose I was just so grateful that somebody, anybody, wanted me, me, a grumpy, illiterate fourteen year old. I love my parents so much that I would do anything to make them happy. I oblige them, whatever the cost, and along the way, I believe that cost has been me.

"And then, there you are, dressed as a man being physically thrown out of an election because you believed in something so passionately that you were willing to risk your freedom for it. Where does one find such passion?" Kit asked, bewildered.

Olivia had noticed Kit's obvious obedient devotion to his father, but she had not expected to learn that in a way, his life had been quite sad.

She saw a likeness between them. Their parents, though total opposites, did not know the true Kit and Olivia.

"What is your goal, Olivia?" Kit asked curiously. "What do you hope to achieve?"

Olivia had not ever been asked that question before. Never. People had always been too busy criticising her actions to ever wonder about her ambitions. Not even Aunt Lorna.

"I want to live in a society where I may be seen just as you saw me a few minutes ago," replied Olivia softly. "A peer." She smiled. "You cannot know what that meant to me, Kit."

Both Kit and Edward looked quite shocked. Neither of them had realised the meaning behind the word.

"I want to see women encouraged to pursue skills and experiences outside the domestic home. I want to see everyone, not just women, educated to the highest level that the government can provide. I want to see girls benefiting from their gender, and not being oppressed because of it. At the present time, we only have one purpose, one future offered to us, but there is more to life than being a wife and a mother. Girls should have the ability to choose another path if they wish. I want to create those paths, lay the stones myself, and hold their hands along the way." Olivia took a deep breath. "And if you are a genie granting me my wishes, I might also ask for a woman prime minister, but then I know you will think I am delusional. But this is what I want to see, and I really do not have any idea of how to achieve it. Which is why I keep frequenting gaols."

Kit and Edward stared at Olivia. They did not seem angry or critical, merely shocked. They would have never heard such ideas before.

Edward was the first to speak. "My sister would like you," he decided. "Alice is clever like you are. I might not understand your predicament, milady, but I have been around a clever enough woman to know they ought to be respected an admired."

Edward was not laughing at her, or dismissing her beliefs. It was a first, and she was incredibly relieved by it. "Thank you, Mr Smith," she said gratefully.

Kit was still silent. He looked terribly conflicted. His brow was tense and his shoulders were stiff. His eyes had not left her. Olivia found his gaze intimidating. She had had to defend her beliefs on numerous occasions. It was a first for her not to be laughed out of a room. Olivia had always had a thick skin. It was rare that anybody was able to get to her.

But that flutter of nerves surfaced again as she anxiously awaited Kit's verdict. She cared what he thought of her, and Olivia did not enjoy the feeling. She was not supposed to care what anyone thought.

"I attended a first rate university for four years, and not once did I have a professor offer me an ounce of the passion that you have just displayed," Kit said, astonished. He shook his head and pinched the bridge of his nose. "People are so self-serving. There are not enough people left, especially not those in power, who care enough about their neighbours. That was what I enjoyed so much about teaching at my mother's school. I was helping children who would otherwise go through life at a disadvantage. I knew exactly what it was to feel less than because of my illiteracy. It was important. I felt as though I was doing something important."

"Why did you stop?" asked Olivia.

"Because ..." Kit stopped himself. He frowned, annoyed. "Because my father wanted me to go to university."

It was truly dawning on Kit just how much he had given up for his parents without even realising. Olivia was certain that her aunt and Cassian had no idea of the pressure Kit felt in order to please them.

"You once told me you were going to change the world," recalled Kit. "I distinctly remember there was no doubt in your conviction. There were no ifs. You were going to change the world. Is that still your plan?"

"Of course," replied Olivia. Olivia most certainly wanted to change the world. It had always been the plan to leave it in a better state then when she had entered it. Only she was at a loss on how to succeed. "I have only failed several dozen times."

"Then let me help you," insisted Kit. "I have only ever felt fulfilment once before, and surely two heads are better than one when changing the world is the plan."

Edward chuckled. "What a pity it was not your name on the ballot today, Kit. Then you could have really made a start in your plans."

What was surely meant to be a joke, had just given Olivia the most brilliant plan. She was a woman fighting in a man's world. It would never work. It was like talking to a deaf man.

She needed to fight fire with fire. She needed the help of a man. She need a male voice, a champion. And what better voice than that of an MP, one who could broach the issues with parliament, and fight for the rights of the people.

Olivia was so excited. As she looked up at Kit, she could see on his face that he had the same idea. While she was eager, he looked apprehensive. "What do you think?" she asked him.

"Me, an MP?" he asked, uncertain.

"Of course! Kit, people like you belong in parliament! Not self-serving braggarts like Sir John Strachan." She hoped that leech had not been re-elected. "You would advocate for the people, and not take advantage of them."

Olivia had already started planning in her head. She knew there was a process to this, and it needed to be done properly.

"I want to help people," Kit said with conviction. "I want to make a difference in the lives of people who are just like I was. I suppose parliament would allow me a platform to do so."

Olivia beamed.

"I suppose I will need to stay in the background then," said Edward. "I must be seen to be above politics."

"Why?" Olivia asked without thinking.

"Because of my father's job, milady. He cannot be seen taking sides when it comes to political parties."

Olivia was utterly confused. "What sort of job would prevent your father from having a political allegiance?"

Edward grinned deviously. "King."

"King?" repeated Olivia. King? What did he mean? Realisation suddenly dawned on her, and she felt utterly stupid. Edward's father was the King. Britain's sovereign. The son of the King was sitting in her drawing room. His Royal Highness Prince Edward was sitting on her settee without a refreshment because Olivia had neglected to offer him one.

In the most ungraceful manner, Olivia fell off the settee and onto her knees, bowing her head. She felt completely ridiculous. How had she not realised? Kit had been so cruel as not to tell her who their guest really was. "Forgive my ignorance, Your Royal Highness."

Edward chuckled. "Do not fuss, Lady Olivia," he said, referring to her correctly, as he was now above her station. "I apologise for the deception. I am incognito, you see."

That explained his attire.

Olivia got up awkwardly and returned to the settee, knowing full well her cheeks were crimson red. "So, an MP?" she chirped, attempting to change the subject.

Chapter 6

Kit had never entertained the idea of his life taking an alternate course. He was always supposed to return home to help his father run the textile business. That was what his life would be. And so he had never imagined what else he could be if he had the freedom to choose.

Kit's start in life had been miserable. He was named for the day he was found. It was highly likely that July twenty-fifth was not his true birthday. Christopher was not the name his first mother had given him. He was raised in a home with dozens of other children and was never afforded an ounce of genuine affection.

In fact, Kit had never felt like he mattered until Cassian had offered him the opportunity to learn to read. Kit had always believed that people like him were not important. It was a common understanding.

And how was that right? Was not it the responsibility of one's elected representatives to advocate for those who did not have a voice?

Kit would not wish the feelings of such insignificance on anyone. It was a harrowing and empty existence. He was going to do something about it.

Kit was going to become an MP. He was going to represent a county or borough fairly and he would do his best to hold himself accountable to the needs of the people. It was important for someone to be elected that knew the plight of the everyday Englishman and woman.

Was this how Olivia felt all the time? Kit had such a rush of energy. It was as though purpose was flowing through his veins.

Olivia's cheeks were still red having just learned of Edward's deception. How shocking it must have been to suddenly realised royalty had graced one's hall. His own mother had reacted quite the same when she had first become acquainted with Edward. It was odd now, really how accustomed he had become in having a prince as a friend.

Kit had to admit that the red was quite becoming on Olivia. Her passion and focus could be construed as a little intimidating. But underneath it, she was still a human girl, and Kit found her to be just as extraordinary as the girl she was in conversation.

"How do I go about this?" Kit asked. There was a hint of embarrassment in his voice. He wanted to be an MP, but had no idea, really, of how to enter the House of Commons.

"You essentially buy your way in," replied Edward, who pursed his lips distastefully. "There is a reason why those who sit in parliament are all sons of peers, or corrupt gentlemen out to sway the majority towards their own interests. Anyone with money can have a say in government these days."

Kit's heart immediately sank. Perhaps it was naïve of him to think he could triumph because he was good.

"Yes, it is true money has a say in things," retorted Olivia, "but anyone with property worth forty shillings or more can vote in an election Kit. If you are able to persuade them towards your cause then you have just as good a chance as any."

Kit had witnessed his father conduct many business transactions. There was always give and take involved. He would have to represent all the people, including the rich, and so he would need to understand what they required of him, whilst not compromising his advocating for the poor.

"I understand it is not my business, but you do have an income of six hundred pounds annually, yes?" asked Edward.

Kit frowned. "What does my income matter?" What a highly inappropriate topic to discuss.

"It matters because MP's must have an income of six hundred pounds a year to represent a county. Do you have such funds?"

Kit did not know why, but he felt very uncomfortable revealing his income in front of Olivia. Olivia seemed nonchalant. Such things, obviously, did not matter to her, and he admired her all the more for it.

"I am one of the owners of my father's estate, Norwood Cottage, and as such I draw a sufficient income from it." Kit cleared his throat awkwardly. "Above six hundred a year." Closer to a thousand a year, though Cassian had intended to quadruple that number once Kit had undertaken a significant work load within the factory business. "How is it you are so knowledgeable?" he asked suddenly, changing the subject. "I thought you were meant to be above all this."

"Just because we are meant to be above politics, does not mean that I am ignorant. I did attend Cambridge for a year, you know." Edward smiled, amused.

"Is that how you two know each other?" asked Olivia. "You are school friends?"

"Oh, no, Lady Olivia. Kit, here, is much older than I," gasped Edward.

Kit scoffed. "Three whole years." The nineteen year old prince could show his immaturity at times.

"There was an attempt on my life a few months ago," Edward explained seriously. "Kit came to my rescue. Surely you read it in the papers? My father knighted him. The he promptly went back to favouring the good son." He murmured the last part under his breath. Kit was unsure if Olivia had caught it.

She did not seem to. "Oh, my. Knighted?" She seemed very impressed. Kit enjoyed the expression on her face. It seemed to take a lot to impress someone like Olivia. "No, I did not know of it. You must have been very brave."

Kit felt almost childlike with the giddy sense of accomplishment he felt at receiving Olivia's approval. To have in his possession her good opinion seemed like an achievement of its own.

Olivia's blue eyes surveyed him as she offered him a warm, satisfied smile. She cocked her head a little to the side and said, "If your beliefs do not see you elected, your decent character will. You have such an opportunity." Kit could have been wrong, but he could have sworn he heard the slightest hint of envy in her tone, but he promptly dismissed it.

Before Kit and Edward departed Olivia's home, the three agreed to keep their ears to the ground to decide on a seat worth standing for. Kit would need to scour his father's newspaper in the morning.

He would also need to tell his father the good, or rather bad, news.

"I wish you luck. I am sure your parents will know what good you can do," Olivia said as she farewelled them. Her small hand reached out and she placed it in his forearm supportively.

Kit caught and held her gaze. He could see the belief in her eyes. They looked just as strong and determined as they did when Olivia would speak about justice. Knowing that someone as strong as Olivia believed in him made him all the more determined to succeed. He did not want to let her down.

Moments later, Olivia removed her hand timidly, and so Kit caught it in his and offered her a firm handshake. Kit loved the feeling of her small hand in his. Kit liked her strong, passionate personality. It separated her from every woman he had ever encountered. But the size of her hand, the flush of her cheeks, and the fleeting glimpses of her bashful side gave him glimpses into her soft, vulnerable side.

Vulnerabilities and insecurities were normal, and Kit was curious to learn more about the Olivia underneath. Perhaps he had the ability to help Olivia, to know her, and to even share her burdens if she wished it.

Olivia seemed to snap out of her shyness as she shook Edward's hand as well.

The two men then departed Olivia's home. It was now dark, the light of the full moon above them lighting their way.

"I must say," remarked Edward as they rode, "I have never encountered a more handsome girl in my life."

Kit had never experienced real jealousy before, but he suddenly felt the urge to punch Edward in the throat. Was that jealousy?

"Such lovely red hair, and a very pretty face. Fine figure, too."

Kit felt his heart beat increase as his anger rose. Edward was not five feet from him. Kit was certain if he leapt from his own horse's back he could take the prince down with him.

Kit did not like Edward commenting on Olivia's appearance. Not only did it bother him that another man noticed her appearance, it bothered him that Olivia's appearance seemed to be the only thing Edward had noticed.

However, the primal side of him was more concerned about the former. Kit wanted to punch Edward in the throat.

Edward laughed. "I can practically smell the ire radiating off of you."

"Are you vexing me on purpose?" Kit demanded to know. "There is so much more to Olivia then her hair or her face. She is ... she is ..." What was the right word?

"Yours?" guessed Edward.

Yes, that was it!

Kit frowned. "No, no," he scolded himself. "Olivia does not belong to me. I would wager she would not want to belong to anyone." Kit could not say that he knew Olivia well, inside and out, but he could tell that she was not the type of girl to be lost in a man.

For what a shame, because Kit was growing more certain that he was the type of man who could be lost in a woman.

"Perhaps you need spectacles, my friend," teased Edward, "because she was looking at you with quite the dazzled expression. I would wager she likes you more than you think."

Kit said nothing further. He only smiled to himself, hoping that Edward was right.

Even if Edward was wrong, and Olivia only wanted to be Kit's ally in this endeavour, that would be perfectly alright with him. Olivia had helped Kit to find himself in just a few short hours. Kit had woken up this morning lost, and unknowingly so. The purpose, inspiration, and fulfilment that he was currently feeling was quite addicting.

"What are you going to tell your father?" asked Edward.

Kit's mood suddenly deflated a little. The look of disappointment on his father's face would undoubtedly be one of the most difficult things Kit would ever have to face. Knowing that in itself made Kit realise just how much he had sacrificed to please his parents. He prayed that Cassian would support his decision.

"I have no idea," replied Kit honestly. "I have never had to tell him anything like this before. I have never disagreed with him, or gone against him. Do you have any advice?"

Edward laughed half-heartedly. "My area of expertise is certainly not getting one's father to understand one's life choices. If you would like some advice on how to get your father to think you are a stone in his shoe, then please, listen to me."

Kit winced.

"Just tell your father the absolute truth. You want to work for the people, and not for him. Trust that he is a better father than mine," offered Edward.

Kit knew that Edward was talking sense. Even though Kit had always appeased his father, he never doubted that Cassian loved him.

The moonlight shone on Norwood Cottage in the distance. Kit took a deep, apprehensive breath. "Please understand, Father," he prayed under his breath.

Chapter 7

By the time that Kit and Edward and returned their horses to the stable, and had watered and wiped them down, the household had long retired.

Kit thought about waking his father up. Perhaps Cassian might be more responsive to the idea if he was not entirely conscious. He knew that was cowardly and decided to wait until morning.

Edward retired to the guest bedroom and Kit did the same.

Kit surprisingly slept well despite the weight on his conscience. He was awoken the next morning by the feeling of someone poking his temple. Seconds later, there was something pressing on his chest, about the weight of a six year old girl.

Kit's eyes opened to see his two younger sisters watching him, with wide, uncertain eyes. They were still wearing their night gowns, and their dark hair was fixed in rags to control their curls.

Emma had climbed atop Kit's chest, while Lucy had climbed on the bed beside him. In seeing the wariness on their face, Kit sat up, shuffling Emma gently off of him and beside Lucy.

Perhaps it was the age difference between himself and the girls, but Kit felt such a sense of duty towards them. It was his job to protect them. They depended on him, as much as they did Cassian. Lucy in particular. Her need would only grow as she ventured out into society. Kit feared the day she would fully comprehend just how cruel people could be.

"What is it, girls?" asked Kit worriedly.

"The doctor just arrived," answered Lucy.

"Mama says Papa is going to have an operation," added Emma.

Doctor Ward was early. Would this mean the scheduled operation would be earlier? Kit was not a doctor, and he had no idea of such things, but he was to understand that the procedure itself was quite simple. The risks thereafter were more worrying. Infection was deadly.

"Why does Papa need an operation?" pressed Emma, a sweet frown line forming between her brows.

Kit knew that the girls knew little of their mother's past, and even less about the circumstances surrounding their move to Derbyshire, and Cassian and Faith's marriage. They would find out eventually, but it was not Kit's story to tell.

"Because ... because he has a sore right here," Kit explained, tapping the right side of Emma's chest. "And Doctor Ward has kindly agreed to fix it for him."

A selfish thought popped into Kit's head. If Doctor Ward had arrived earlier than scheduled, and the operation would be brought forward, it meant that it would be highly the wrong time to bring up the subject of Kit abandoning the family business. Cassian would need Kit now more than ever to look after his mother and sisters whilst he was indisposed.

"It must be worse than a sore, Kit," decided Lucy. "Mama would not be so worried otherwise," she deduced.

Lucy might have only been ten, but she was very astute. This perceptiveness would only hurt her in years to come.

"Well, if Mother is so worried then you ought not to be bothering me about it. Should you not be trying to make her morning a little easier? What might she like? A tidy nursery perhaps? Off with you," he dismissed playfully.

Lucy and Emma ran from his bedroom in the direction of the nursery. Tidying would keep them occupied for an hour or two. It was never clean. Kit heard Cat's bark in the hallway as the little dog followed them.

Kit climbed out of bed and quickly dressed. He collected his father's golden pocket watch from the dressing table and ran his hand through his hair by way of combing it.

Compared to the level of excitement and inspiration he was feeling yesterday, Kit suddenly felt much deflated. It was as though he had been dreaming and he had just woken up to his reality.

Not only that, an unsettling feeling of guilt had begun to surface. How selfish was he to be thinking about himself when his father was about to undergo a serious surgical procedure.

He was selfish enough to want to leave this house to go and visit Olivia once more. The feeling he had while being around her was infectious. When with Olivia, Kit felt like he could do anything, achieve everything.

But here, Kit felt stunted, and once again, he hated the selfishness. He was unused to being selfish. He supposed he would have to get used to it.

Kit went downstairs. The foyer was abandoned, but the drawing room door was closed. The house was always open in the morning, so it meant that room was occupied. As he approached the door, he could hear the voices of his parents inside, and the voice of a man he did not recognise. It had to be Doctor Ward.

"What are we doing?"

Edward's hushed voice made Kit jump. He had not heard his friend descend the stairs, nor had he realised that his ear was practically at the keyhole. Kit stood up straight.

"My father's surgeon is in there," replied Kit in a hushed tone.

"Surgeon?" Edward frowned. "Is everything alright?"

"Yes, yes, it was scheduled." Kit then noticed Edward was unusually dressed for the morning. He was wearing a travelling cloak and a hat. He looked as though he had somewhere to be. Kit subsequently saw the letter in Edward's hand.

"Alice," Edward explained. "She writes telling me my father has found out I have no intention of returning to Cambridge. He is none too pleased." Edward pressed his lips firmly together, indicating the language in the letter was a little more colourful. "I must return home to be compared to the good son." Edward scoffed, referring to his father's favourite son, Charles. "You will thank your family for their hospitality, won't you? I was hoping to thank them in person but it seems it is not a good time. I have much enjoyed my escape from royal life."

"I will tell them," promised Kit. "Stand up to your father, though," he encouraged, and he could not help the smile the crept across his face. "I know I can talk."

Edward laughed. "Your father loves you. My father barely tolerates me. The outcomes would be severely different, I assure you."

Edward placed a hand on Kit's shoulder. "I will keep my ear to the ground of contestable seats. Give Olivia my best. And good luck, my friend. I cannot wait to hear all about it."

With that, Edward departed Norwood Cottage.

A little while later, the door to the drawing room opened and Cassian, Faith, and Doctor Ward emerged.

"Tomorrow morning, then," said Doctor Ward in a confirmation tone.

"Yes, tomorrow. I am looking forward to getting this thing out of me," replied Cassian.

Faith nearly looked green.

"I will take good care of your husband, Mrs Kensington," promised Doctor Ward. "There is no need to worry."

"I will stop worrying when this is over," said Faith firmly.

"Ah, Kit," said Cassian, noticing that they were not alone in the foyer. "Doctor, allow me to introduce my son, Kit Kensington."

The doctor smiled as Kit extended his hand in greeting. "A pleasure to meet you, Mr Kensington."

"You as well, Doctor Ward," replied Kit.

"Faith, would you see to it that Doctor Ward has something for breakfast? I am sure he is hungry after his journey," suggested Cassian.

Faith nodded, and ushered Doctor Ward in the direction of the dining room.

"If I were not so concerned about Faith's nerves, I would be terrified," confessed Cassian to Kit, now that they were alone.

Kit could see the anxiety on his father's face, though, even as he tried to hide it.

"You look troubled, son. Is something on your mind?"

Kit had not realised he was wearing his turmoil so obviously on his face. "Worried about you," he lied. Awful! Of course he was worried about his father, but that was not what his turmoil was regarding.

Cassian smiled. "Doctor Ward just explained the procedure to us. It is simple, according to him. Are you sure there isn't anything else that is troubling you? You seem awfully peculiar this morning."

Yes, Father. I want to tell you that I have decided to throw away the four years of schooling you have just paid for. I do not want to go into business with you. I have no desire to manage your textile factories. I want to help people, and I plan on doing that by becoming an elected MP. I have never, not once, made a decision that would suit me, and this is what I want to do, no matter how disappointed in me you must be.

Oh, and Olivia Pendleton is going to help me do it.

Kit looked directly into his father's eyes and lied. "No." Was that not some mortal sin?

Cassian was asking him if something was on his mind and Kit could not bring himself to confess. He was a coward.

Cassian seemed to accept Kit's answer. "Alright then. I wanted to ask you for your help anyway. It seems I am going to be bedridden for a time afterward. I need you to look after my correspondence for me in this time. Answer my letters, approve wages, deal with enquiries and the like. It will be good practice for you."

Perhaps Finn would be a better choice, Father. I had really hoped to get a start on researching contestable seats. I thought I might call on Olivia today and we might do it together.

"Of course," Kit agreed. Coward.

Cassian grinned. "I knew I could count on you," he said proudly. "Come on. We will start on today's together so that you will be confident going forth on your own."

His father's proud tone was almost as addicting as Olivia's infectious passion. Almost. Kit loved that his father was proud of his choice, but Kit knew he was only biding time.

Cassian led Kit up the stairs, and with every step Kit's feet felt heavier, as though someone was pulling him back. Would he ever have the courage to disappoint his father?

Cassian spent the rest of the day giving Kit instructions for the correspondence. Cassian had specific ways of wanting things answered. Kit took notes, and with every scrape of the quill against the parchment, he felt what little confidence he had leaving him. This was to be his reality if he did not do something about it.

"This is what I always wanted for us, you know," Cassian remarked happily. "After all these years, we have gone from reading lessons in my study to actually working together. You cannot fathom how proud I am of you, Kit."

It was like a knife to the heart.

Chapter 8

Kit did not know which was more harrowing. The fact that his father lay unconscious in bed, or the fact that a lead bullet lay in a dish beside him on the bedside table.

The surgery had gone flawlessly according to Doctor Ward. Despite the fact that there was quite a lot of scar tissue as a result of the time between the original injury and the operation, Doctor Ward was able to locate the bullet and remove it with as minimal invasiveness as possible.

Cassian's breathing and heartrates were steady, and he would wake up in good time. But that had not prevented Kit from imagining the worst. What if the surgery had gone wrong? God forbid, what if Cassian had died? What if the last thing he had ever told his father was a lie?

Kit knew that he needed to tell his parents the truth no matter the consequences. He did not know if he could endure their disappointment, after all, he had never disappointed them before.

Kit looked up at Faith. She was sitting on the opposite side of Cassian's bed, staring at her husband's chest, watching as it rose and fell. Her shoulders were still incredibly tense as there were intent frown lines between her brows as she concentrated.

"Are you able to relax yet, Mother?" Kit asked her.

Faith's concentration broke as she looked to Kit. Upon meeting his eyes, her shoulders did relax a little and she offered him a small smile.

"I shall as soon as he wakes," she replied. "You have been such a help to us this summer, Kit," she said sincerely. "It has been such a dreaded time in our lives, and you have made it easier on us. Particularly where your sisters are concerned." Faith looked at him sympathetically. "I know this should have been a more special time for you. We are both so terribly proud of you for what you have achieved. First with Cambridge, and then your bravery concerning the prince. You really ought to have been in London for the season, enjoying all that comes with receiving one of the king's honours, but instead you have been here." Faith used her sleeve to wipe away the tears that had begun to pool in her eyes. "You cannot know what it means to me to have a son I can watch grow and thrive."

Kit was hearing such wonderful, loving words from his mother, and all he felt was guilt. Had he let it go on too long? Ought he to have been more rebellious over the years? Was it too late now?

Kit did not care about missing the parties he would have been invited to had he spent the summer in London. He was happy to support his parents and look after his sisters during this time. But he knew that when Faith referred to him growing and thriving, she was referring to what she and Cassian intended for him.

What felt even worse was that Faith felt even more blessed to have him having lost her first born son. It was not a subject often mentioned in the Kensington household. At least, not to Kit and his sisters. But Kit knew what had happened. And everyone knew who Faith's special place in the garden was for.

Kit took a deep breath, knowing he could only ask. "What if I did something to disappoint you?" he asked quietly.

Faith frowned. "Whatever do you mean?"

"What if I did something to disappoint you?" Kit repeated. "Would you still be proud of me? Would you still love me?"

Faith still looked positively puzzled. "What an odd question, Kit. Nothing you could ever do would stop us from loving you."

Kit stared into his mother's kind, yet concerned, brown eyes. This woman was his mother, not by birth, but in every other way. She, along with Cassian, had given him the family that he had always craved. Kit trusted Faith. If she said that his actions would not change the way she felt about him then he had to trust that.

"I need to tell you something," he murmured.

Faith looked quite uncertain. "What?" she asked nervously.

Kit looked cautiously to his father. He still appeared as though he was out cold. His attention returned to Faith. "I realised ... yesterday ... that I have never made a decision in my life that would suit me," Kit began slowly.

"I do not understand," Faith said, leaning forward as much as her rounded belly would allow.

"I love you both so much that I have gone along with whatever you wished me to do," Kit continued. "You both wanted me to leave my position at your school, and so I did. You wanted me to go to university, and so I did. You wanted me to study business, and so I did. You wanted me to go into business with Father, and so I intended to." Kit sucked in a breath.

Faith appeared quite concerned. "We agreed that university was the right thing for you, Kit. We agreed that you and Cassian would work together, father and son. You agreed."

"Yes, I did," Kit sighed. "I agreed because I could not bear the thought of either of you being disappointed in me. I want you to be happy with me because you opening your hearts and your home to me all those years ago saved my life.

"But I realised just what I was doing yesterday. I realised I was not passionate about anything and the last thing I wanted to do with my life was sit in Father's office and comb over quarterly reports.

"I thought back to the last time I felt as though I had any passion for what I was doing, and that was when I was teaching. I felt as though I was making a difference in the lives of those children. I was doing good. I was able to improve the prospects of someone far less fortunate than I. I want to do the same thing on a much larger scale." Kit took a deep breath. "It is my ambition to be elected to parliament."

Kit watched Faith for a reaction, but she simply stared at him. All sorts of shock emotions crossed her face. Sadness seemed to settle as the emotion she was feeling.

Kit felt sick. He felt physically ill. Oh, Lord. What had he just done? Disappointment. Here it came. Kit was not prepared for it.

"I cannot believe that you are two and twenty and yet I know so little of your heart, Kit," Faith said quietly. Her eyes were glassy, as though she was about to cry. "How is it we have made you to feel as though you must comply with our wishes to earn our love?"

Kit recoiled. Faith did not seem to be upset with him. She was upset with herself.

"I want you to live your very best life, Kit. If that was working with Cassian then I would support it wholeheartedly. But if it is working for the people, then I will support that, too."

She meant it. Had Kit worked himself up over nothing? Kit leapt out of his chair and was around to Faith's side of the room in seconds. Faith stood up as Kit hugged her tightly. She laughed tearfully as she returned the gesture.

"Never feel as though you need to earn our love, Kit," urged Faith. "I curse myself for not recognising that you felt this way. I feel as though I have failed to make you feel as one of our own. Lucy and Emma certainly do not always follow instructions."

"No," retorted Kit, pulling away from her. "I have never felt excluded or unloved. I have known a wonderful life here. I suppose I am eternally grateful to you and Father for giving me the greatest gift I could ever receive."

Faith placed her hands on Kit's shoulders and looked him in the eye. "I see you now, Kit. I see a different side to you. But I know the caring, supporting foundation remains. If being an MP is important to you, then we shall endeavour to support you in any way we can."

Kit heard the sincerity in his mother's voice, and he felt the conviction in her promise, but there was a small part of him that could not fully be comfortable.

He still had to tell his father.

And the small matter of Olivia's involvement had yet to be broached.

Kit and Faith mutually agreed to wait until Cassian was back to full strength before they told him the truth about Kit's future plans.

He had awoken the following afternoon in a lot of pain. Doctor Ward was helping Cassian to manage it using pain remedies. The doctor was also monitoring Cassian closely for infection and fever.

Kit had been taking care of his father's business for a week now. Cassian was healing well, but he was still resting in bed. Doctor Ward had left the day before, and had left Faith instructions for Cassian's continued care.

Cassian was able to move around the bedroom for short times, but he was still experiencing pain in his chest and restrictions in his arm and shoulder movement.

Kit had underestimated just how much his father did for work. Cassian had hired two managers for the northern and southern factories, but Cassian was still the overall head of the business. He oversaw everything. From workers' wages to the price of fabric bolts, Cassian handled it all.

If it were possible, Kit had gained even more respect for his father. Cassian had built his company from nothing. He had built himself from nothing. It was possible to rise in the world with the right ambition, and just a little help from kind people.

Cassian's help had come from Faith.

Kit's help had come from Cassian.

Kit wanted to do the same thing for so many more.

Kit used Cassian's seal to approve the sale of a new shipment of cotton and placed it in the pile of letters that needed to be sent out.

Kit respected his father, but Lord his work was dull. If Kit had to read the word "cotton" one more time he would use the letter knife to scratch his eyes out.

Before Kit could move on to the next banal document, there was a knock on the study door.

"Yes?" he prompted.

Mr Wade entered the study, followed closely by Olivia. She wore a heavy, hooded cloak, which was an odd choice of garment considering it was still summer. "A Miss Smith to see you, Mr Kensington."

Kit smiled and stood up from the desk. Miss Smith? "Thank you, Wade."

Mr Wade bowed his head and departed the study.

Olivia pushed back her hood to reveal that her cheeks were nearly as red as her hair, which was quite untidy after having a hood over it for the journey. She looked quite warm. She then discarded the cloak on the back of the chair before Cassian's desk.

"I thought it prudent to travel incognito. You can thank Prince Edward for the idea. I have a feeling I would not be welcome in this house if I used my true name."

Kit's smile faded. He knew his parents would have difficulty in accepting his developing relationship with Olivia purely because her last name was Pendleton.

Olivia placed her hands on her hips. Even though her face was red, she looked beautiful and healthy. "I can forgive you for not writing me once. But twice?" Her tone was comical and her smile was wry, but Kit knew he had left her without news for over a week.

Kit walked around the desk and invited Olivia to sit down on the chairs that sat before it. "I apologise. It had been quite the week here at Norwood."

"Is everything alright?" Olivia frowned.

"I am sure you remember how my father was shot several years ago."

Kit saw the haunted look flash through Olivia's blue eyes. "Oh, yes. I could never forget. I witnessed it."

Kit could not imagine what such a sight would be for a child. What were Olivia's parents thinking allowing her to be present? Then again, from what he had heard over the years, Olivia's parents were not the best of people.

"He had the bullet removed this week. He is convalescing," explained Kit.

"But he will be well?" checked Olivia.

Kit nodded. "Yes, no infection or fever. Just a little pain now."

"Well, I am glad it went well," Olivia said sincerely. "It must have been very frightening for your family." Olivia extended her arm and placed her hand on top of his.

Olivia's hand was warm and comforting. Kit looked up from her hand and met Olivia's eyes. Having leant over to offer him her hand, Olivia's face was much closer to him. She looked just as nervous and he felt.

Olivia's blue eyes were wide as she stared at him. Her lips parted slightly and Kit could hear the quickening of her breath. Olivia, for the first time in their short acquaintance, looked vulnerable.

What Kit would have done to close the distance between them, but he knew it would not be right. It would be taking advantage.

Before Kit could do the gentlemanly thing and move away, the door to the study was opened once more, this time without the courtesy of a knock.

"Kit, I wanted to see how you were getting on –" Cassian, who was being supported by Faith, stopped dead in their tracks as they took in the scene before them.

Recognition flooded Faith's face as she stared at Olivia. Ire flooded Cassian's as he glared at Kit.

Chapter 9

"Olivia?" gasped Faith. "Can it be?"

"Hello, Aunt Anne," Olivia greeted quietly as she stood from her chair.

Kit saw his mother flinch at the sound of what was once her name. She had not been Anne for many, many years. This negative reaction, slight as it was, made Cassian all the more angry.

Kit did not feel apologetic, however. He felt protective. It seemed instinctual to place himself between Cassian and Olivia. His father's prejudice towards her purely because her surname was Pendleton was now ridiculous.

"I thought I made my position on this subject clear, Kit," Cassian said firmly. He was doing well to control his tone. "She was not to come anywhere near your mother. What is she doing here?" he demanded to know.

Kit's eyes narrowed. "Olivia is not here to see Mother," he retorted. Kit had never spoken to his father with even the slightest tone of contempt. But he could not simply stand by and let Olivia be treated as such, no matter what his father thought.

Kit suddenly realised that he cared more about Olivia's honour than he did his father's rules.

"She is here as my guest," Kit continued.

"Perhaps I ought to leave..." Olivia said quietly.

"Please. Don't," Kit instructed, holding out his hand, his eyes not leaving his father's. Cassian's eyes were naturally black, which only made them seem all the more angry when he was glaring at Kit in such a way.

Faith helped Cassian to sit down on the wooden chair that was situated beside the door of the study. She still looked positively shocked to see Olivia. Perhaps they had not seen each other since Olivia was a child.

"You understood why such an attachment could not continue, Kit," Cassian said intensely. "You promised me that you would never enter into such an attachment. You understood why I could never allow for one of the Pendletons to be brought back into your mother's life."

Kit understood his father's deep need to protect Faith from anything and everything. Faith came first in Cassian's eyes, and Kit respected the deep love that his parents had for each other. Kit understood the threat Cassian saw from the Pendletons, but he had never verbally promised to stay away from Olivia. Perhaps he had known on some level that he would never be able to keep such a promise.

"What on earth are you talking about?" Faith asked Cassian impatiently.

Cassian ignored her, his ire still focussed on Kit. "How could you deliberately disobey in this way?" Cassian sounded deeply betrayed, and that tone felt like a knife wound.

Before Kit could respond, Olivia had stepped around him. Olivia's hands were on her hips and she had determination in his eyes. Kit should have known better than to think Olivia needed his protection.

"Mr Kensington, I would appreciate it if you would not refer to my surname as though it reflects my character," she snapped.

Cassian did not back down. "You are inconsequential, my dear, and I do not mean any offense. For your surname includes your parents, and any involvement you have with my son only invites those people back into my wife's life, which is something I will never allow." Cassian's attention returned to Kit. "I thought my son understood that."

Kit winced.

"Cassian," Faith said firmly, interrupting the conversation. "I feel I am missing a key piece of information here, but I will not have you dismissing Olivia on my behalf." Faith smiled fondly at Olivia. "She is my niece, after all."

Olivia returned Faith's kind smile. She then turned to Cassian. "Kit respects you more than you know, Mr Kensington."

"I have a feeling I know what this is about," continued Faith. "Why don't we all sit down, and Kit, you can tell us everything. I am sure once it is all out in the open there will be no reason for quarrelling."

Kit nodded, agreeing. He collected the chair from behind Cassian's desk, and he, Olivia, and Faith helped to position those chairs around Cassian, so that they were sitting in a circle.

Cassian still looked very much put out. His eyes were narrow and dark, and his lips were pressed into a firm line. His hands were sitting on his knees and his posture was rigid and stiff.

Kit felt very conflicted as he began to find the words to explain himself to his father. He had so feared disappointing Cassian. But now, in Cassian's eyes, Kit had betrayed him. Which was worse? Betrayal. It was an absurd overreaction, but Kit could never betray his father. Disappointing him was preferable.

"When I first met Olivia, years ago when we travelled to Leicestershire, I had never encountered a girl with more conviction or passion for what she believed in. Olivia was determined to change the world. She knew exactly how to do it, and she did not care what obstacles she had to climb." Kit offered her a fond smile. "And when I spoke to her in the gaol, and in every conversation since, I have been astounded by the continued compassion she feels for the underprivileged masses, in particular her support for women. It made me realise that I had never experienced such drive. I was not passionate about the direction in which my life was headed. Olivia helped me to realise that I had the power and the opportunity to change my mind, and to choose the path that I felt would help me to make a difference.

"When we voted in the election, we were choosing the lesser of two evils. Both were corrupt in different ways. It has become the norm that those who represent us in parliament are self-serving snakes who pass and deny bills and reforms to line their own pockets." Kit took a deep breath as he made determined eye contact with his father. "I have only felt as though I was contributing to society once in my life, and that was when I was teaching at Mother's school. I have decided to become an MP. I want to sit in parliament and create reform that benefits the people. I want to do something that matters. I want to ... I want to change the world." Kit used Olivia's words, but they were perfect.

"And that was what I came here today to tell you, Kit," added Olivia. "I received word that a county seat in Hertfordshire is to be decided on by Christmas. It is currently held by a Whig and so the Tories are eager for a win."

Kit grinned. Hertfordshire. So it would be.

"Despite the questions that I have surrounding gaol conversations, I think you will make a wonderful MP, Kit," Faith said sincerely.

"Thank you, Mother," Kit said gratefully.

Faith placed her hand on Cassian's forearm, encouraging him to offer his blessing as well.

Cassian was quiet for a minute before he spoke. Taking a deep breath, he said, "I cannot fathom your logic here, Kit. I am quite honestly shocked. I am shocked that you could so deliberately disobey me in continuing to see Olivia. You know what pain they caused!" At the use of the word 'they', Cassian pointed at Olivia.

"Olivia was not responsible for any of that!" Kit said defensively.

"You are missing my point!" exclaimed Cassian. "You know what pain they caused and yet you still made the decision to bring them back into our lives. I thought you were mature enough to comprehend the responsibility of family. How could you be so selfish?"

"That is quite enough, both of you!" Faith cried, but she was ignored once more.

That word struck a nerve and Kit flinched. "Selfish?" he repeated angrily. "You think me selfish?" Kit could feel his ire bubbling to the surface. Suppressed feelings and were threatening to explode from his mouth, just like a volcano. "I have never, not once, made a decision to suit myself. I always consider my family, and I have always decided to make the choice you think is best for me. I went to the school you told me to attend. I studied what you told me to study. I came home when you told me to. I looked after the girls when you needed me to. I was going to go into business with you, just to please you!" Kit shouted. He was out of his seat, pacing, huffing and puffing as years of stifled emotions seemed to escape his lips. "I have done everything in my power to make you proud of me from the second you gave me your name. Don't you dare call me selfish."

Cassian snorted. "I did not realise it made me such a poor father to want the best for you. I did everything in my power to give you the best, Kit," Cassian shouted back in retort. "And yet all I receive in return are lies. I will not have you threatening this family! I will not have those people in our lives!"

Kit saw red. "You are the one who is threatening this family!" he roared. "All I ever wanted was to please you and the minute I make a decision to suit my own happiness it is betrayal."

Kit needed to get out. He needed to leave before he did something stupid. He could see in his father's eyes that Cassian believed himself to be right. There would be no changing his mind.

Kit, in his anger, wanted to injure his father. "Perhaps you should have chosen a more obedient orphan to be your son," he seethed.

Cassian shut his mouth as he stared at Kit.

"Kit!" Faith cried. She sounded as though she was about to cry, and so Kit could not look at her.

"I need to go," Kit said dejectedly. He marched past his parents and pulled open the study door with such force that he nearly damaged the hinges.

Lucy and Emma jumped away from the door. They had clearly been listening at the keyhole.

"Kit, what's wrong?" Lucy begged.

Kit's strides were quick as he made his way down the corridor towards his bedroom. Olivia had left the study and was following him. His sisters were running alongside him, trying to keep up.

"Kit, do not leave it like that," urged Olivia. "Angry words were exchanged but he is still your father. He loves you."

Kit was too angry to think coherently. All he could manage to comprehend was that he needed to leave this house. He had a destination. Hertfordshire. He had an election to win.

Kit rounded on Olivia, stopping right in the middle of the hall. He stared down at her intensely. Kit could see the sympathy in her eyes, but he was too riled up to appreciate the good place her heart was in. "Are you coming with me, or not?" he asked her.

"To Hertfordshire?"

"I need you, Olivia. I cannot do it without you."

Olivia nodded earnestly. "Of course I will come with you, but I really think you ought to –"

"No. I have nothing further to say to him," he said dismissively. "I am leaving. Immediately."

"Why were you and Papa quarrelling, Kit?" asked Lucy sadly.

"Why is Papa angry?" asked Emma.

Kit's heart immediately softened at the fearful tones expressed by his sisters. They were innocent. He knelt down before them and took one of their tiny hands each in his. "I need to go away for a while," he said quietly. "But I promise I will write you letters. I will send you my address when I have one. Will you write to me?"

Kit was used to being away from his sisters. Four years of schooling had done that. But having been home this summer he had grown used to their enchanting company.

Kit hugged Lucy and Emma tightly as they ambitiously promised to write him every day, while still questioning his reasons for going.

Faith had left the study and was now approaching them. Kit saw her distraught facial expression over Lucy and Emma's shoulders. Her hands were resting on her belly.

Kit felt an immediate pang of guilt for distressing his mother during her pregnancy. The child was one of the reasons why Cassian did not want Faith to know about Olivia.

"Mother ..." Kit trailed off sadly as he stood up.

"You both need to apologise," she insisted. "I know you did not mean it, and neither did Cassian. Just apologise and we can put this behind us. We do not want you to leave!"

"I can't, Mother. I meant what I said." For the most part. The last part was meant to directly injure his father, but he had meant everything else. "I have to go. It is important." It was necessary.

Faith let out a sob as she stood up on her toes and wrapped her arms around Kit's neck, engulfing him in a tight hug. "I do not understand how this has happened."

"I think it would have always happened some time or another, Mother," confessed Kit. Even before Olivia, Kit had been suppressing these emotions. They were bound to surface at some point, creating inevitable friction when they did. "I love you. I will write you."

Faith pulled away. "There isn't anything I can say?" she asked sadly.

Kit shook his head. "This is something I have to do."

Faith nodded in regretful acceptance. She looked over at Olivia, who was standing to the side of them with the girls standing next to her. "It was wrong of me to neglect you, Olivia. You are my niece and I had – have – a duty to care for you."

Olivia offered her aunt a small smile. "It takes a great deal more than neglect to injure me, Aunt Anne – I mean Faith!" she corrected herself.

"I want to get to know you, Olivia. I want to know the person you have become, one day." She sighed, turning back to Kit. "Promise me you will come back," Faith insisted. She gripped Kit's hands as she waited for his answer.

Kit nodded. It would not be goodbye forever. But it was goodbye for now.

Chapter 10

Olivia struggled to keep up with Kit's quick pace as he walked down to the stable. Being so tall, his strides were much longer than hers.

Kit had thrown his valuables and a few spare garments of clothing into a knapsack and that was it. He was ready to leave his home and his family.

Olivia could not say that she knew Kit extraordinarily well. They had developed an odd sort of friendship, but they were yet to get to know one another properly. But in saying that, she could have never predicted that Kit would have this sort of anger inside of him.

Kit was frustrated with his father, and that frustration had brought all sorts of repressed feelings to the surface. Kit and Cassian had exchanged words that Olivia was certain they would regret.

On the one hand, Olivia was proud of Kit. He had never stood up for himself before. Kit had stated what he wanted. He had made the decision to follow his own passion, his own ambition, as opposed to his father's ideas of what was best. Even more than that, he had explained his reasons so beautifully to his parents.

On the other hand, Cassian's reaction had initiated the afore-mentioned unpleasant words exchanged. Cassian had not been able to comprehend what Kit was telling him. Instead, he had been focused on the fact that Kit had continued to see Olivia when he had been instructed not to.

Olivia knew there was bad blood between their families. But she had been a mere child when they had last met. How could Cassian dismiss her without even knowing her? How could she be held accountable for the sins of her parents?

Cassian had said that she was inconsequential, but that was irrelevant. Olivia was guilty by association in his eyes.

Olivia was rarely affected by harsh words. She was used to being called all sorts of colourful names by those who did not understand her choices, but rejection was something that did hurt her.

The wound of rejection never really healed.

"Kit, you really ought to go back there and speak with your father," urged Olivia, who was quickly becoming out of breath as she ran along behind him.

"You heard what he had to say," Kit said dismissively. Olivia could hear the pain in his voice. "I need to go, Olivia. I need to make my own way. I need to be the sort of man someone like you could be proud of."

Olivia stopped in her tracks as a childish smile spread across her face. Kit wanted her respect. He wanted her help on this next adventure. She was valuable to him. Olivia, nor her ideals, had never been much use to anyone.

Reality quickly settled back in and Olivia kept on moving. "Kit, I know you will regret leaving your family like this. I know you love your father!" she called again after him.

It was Kit who stopped in his tracks this time. He turned around and immediately captured her gaze with his intense, blue eyes. He covered the distance between them in seconds, standing only a foot from Olivia as he stared down at her.

"It is true, I do love my father," he confirmed quietly, not breaking eye contact. Olivia held her breath. "All I have ever done, every action, has been to appease my father, to show him my love and respect. I will always be eternally grateful to him. I am not ignorant of where I might be at this moment had he not shown me such kindness. But that does not mean he has the right to dictate my life for me. You, Olivia, have shown me the type of life that I want to lead, an honourable life, and I hope one day my father will accept it, and accept you. But I have no plans to wait around for him to come to that realisation." Kit smiled down at Olivia. "I want you to do this with me, Olivia."

Olivia exhaled. She had been trying to enact change, to make a difference, for years. She had never achieved anything really. She had been mocked, knocked back, and ridiculed more times than she could count. She had frequented half a dozen gaol cells and she had escaped severe punishment by a whisker.

With Kit, Olivia was certain that she could succeed. They could succeed. Kit understood what it was to be poor and uneducated in this country, and he had the money and influence to bring about real change.

No matter how Olivia screamed and shouted, her gender would always be a limitation until someone like Kit was in parliament.

Olivia had the great ability to exert confidence, and appear to others as though she had no insecurities. But she did. She had many, all courtesy of her loving mother. But Kit's faith in her, and his belief in what she stood for, made her feel more powerful than ever.

Everything her mother had ever said, every name and every cold, cruel word, mattered not. She was powerful, and someone believed in her. Kit believed in her. This feeling was intoxicating, and Olivia knew, if she was not careful, that she could easily lose her heart in this fight.

"Olivia?"

Olivia snapped out of her thoughts to find that Kit was still standing just as close to her.

"What were you thinking about so intently?"

"My mother," she answered truthfully.

"Your mother?"

Olivia nodded. Her mother was, and continued to be, a subject of great pain for Olivia. She looked up at Kit with hopeful eyes. "I would like to tell you about our relationship sometime."

Kit softened. "I would like to hear about it," he said sincerely.

"In Hertfordshire," added Olivia, who changed her tone to sound more determined, "after you win."

Kit chuckled. "You are with me?"

Olivia nodded. "Yes, I am with you," she agreed. No truer words had ever escaped her mouth.

Kit and Olivia rode to her grandfather's estate for shelter, so that they could make plans to travel in the morning.

No sooner has they crossed the threshold of Murray Park, Olivia was intercepted by her aunt.

"Olivia!" scolded Lorna. "You really must stop leaving the house without telling me." At that moment, Lorna realised that Olivia was not alone, and her brown eyes went to assess Kit. She recognised him instantly. "Mr Kensington," she greeted suspiciously, "we were not expecting you."

"I apologise for the intrusion, Miss Murray," said Kit.

"Can Kit stay here the night?" Olivia asked. "We will be leaving in the morning," she added almost inaudibly.

But Lorna heard it. She placed her hands on her hips and looked at Olivia as though she were a naughty schoolgirl. "We?" she said icily.

Olivia nodded sheepishly. Her aunt had always been too good to her. Lorna had never truly scolded her, or absolutely forbidden her from doing what she wished. Lorna always told Olivia when she disapproved, but her actions were always Olivia's choice.

"Miss Murray, if I may," interjected Kit. "I have decided to nominate myself to parliament. I will be contesting a county seat in Hertfordshire in the upcoming election near Christmastime. Olivia has agreed to help me. Truly, she is indispensable."

Olivia smiled. She was indispensable.

Lorna arched a brow. "Is he the one standing for election, or are you planning another game of dress-up? Hertfordshire is a lot farther for me to travel to get you out of prison, Olivia."

"Yes, yes," she promised. "Kit is the one who is standing, I swear."

Lorna seemed to accept the truth. "Olivia, you cannot go without a chaperone," she then objected. "And I cannot leave Papa."

Olivia's face fell. "A chaperone? I go out on my own all the time! I have never needed a chaperone!"

"You have always needed a chaperone," Lorna countered, "but I have given you freedom because I have not been able to leave Papa. Olivia, it is far too inappropriate to travel with a man alone. Think of your reputation!"

"Kit is not any ordinary man. He is my friend," insisted Olivia, "and he will protect me. Besides, whatever reputation I had was shattered the first time I was arrested. What do I need it for anyway?"

"Oh, I do not know," said Lorna sarcastically, "a marriage one day?"

Olivia knew her reputation was far too unpredictable for many, many families to want to align themselves with her, not that she cared. Marriage to any one of the hundreds of stiff gentlemen in this country would poison her.

"Well, as I have no intention of marrying, your objection has no grounds," insisted Olivia.

Olivia noticed Lorna's eyes subtly flick between her and Kit, before she pursed her lips in a sort of knowing smile. What was that supposed to mean?

"If you insist," she murmured. "Perhaps you might like to speak to your grandfather first, though. His knowledge of politics might surprise you. He is up in his sitting room." Lorna left them.

Chapter 11

"What is your grandfather like?" asked Kit. "How does he know so much about politics?"

Olivia shrugged her shoulders. In all the time that she had lived here, she had rarely ever seen her grandfather leave his armchair, let alone display in interest in parliament. "I do not know. But he is a dear, dear man. The dearest old man you would ever meet. I do love him very much."

Kit and Olivia climbed the stairs together to find Bernard sitting in his usual armchair, a cup of tea on the table beside him, and today's newspaper in his hands.

Owing to Bernard's increasing deafness, he did not hear them enter the room. Olivia gently tapped her grandfather on the shoulder and then kissed the top of his head.

Bernard craned his neck, and a wide, happy smile spread across his face when he saw it was Olivia that had come to visit him.

"This is a nice surprise," Bernard remarked. He then noticed Kit hovering in the doorway, waiting to be acknowledged before he entered the room. "And who is this?" he asked.

"This is my friend, Kit Kensington, Grandpapa," Olivia introduced. "Kit, this is my grandfather, Bernard Murray, baronet."

Kit smiled nervously as he approached Bernard. He bowed respectfully. "Sir, it is a pleasure to meet you."

"Hello, Kurt," Bernard replied in greeting.

Olivia and Kit exchanged a glance. There was no point in correcting Bernard. It was a miracle that he had heard the 'k' sound. Olivia wondered what her name might have been had Bernard not heard it before his hearing had started to go.

Olivia knelt down beside her grandfather. "Grandpapa, have you any insight on government?" Olivia asked. "Aunt Lorna seemed to think you would."

Bernard's face softened. "Of course you can have a biscuit, darling. There you go." Bernard lifted the tea plate from the table and offered the ginger biscuits to her.

Olivia obliged him and took a biscuit. She then gave one to Kit. "Politics, Grandpapa, politics," she insisted. "Have you any information to offer us?" Olivia noticed a headline in the newspaper that her grandfather had been reading.

Parliament Chaos: MP's Vote on Increasing Grain Cost

"Here, Grandpapa," Olivia urged Bernard to follow her finger as she underlined the word "MP's" with her fingernail.

Bernard read the word, and said, "MP's?"

Olivia nodded, and then pointed at his chest.

Bernard's eyes widened in surprise. "Oh, well I suppose I never did tell you that story. Lorna probably told you about my old days in London, did she?"

Olivia shook her head, exchanging a look of bewilderment with Kit. She had not known that her grandfather had ever spent any time in London. She could not imagine him anywhere other than the chair he was currently occupying.

"Yes, it is true. Your grandfather was once a member of the House of Commons once upon a time."

Olivia sat back on her knees.

"I started with good intentions. I had not the brains for university, but I had the heart for politics, for making changes, you see. I always held those folks in London with high esteem. They were the ones who decided for us. And sometimes those decisions were the wrong ones. I thought I might change them."

Olivia smiled with pride. She loved her dear grandfather, but she now respected him more than ever. Perhaps this was where her ambition had come from? She had inherited her grandfather's wilful spirit.

"My father bought the election for me, of course. I thought nothing of it. It was how things were done. I had my seat in London nonetheless." Olivia's mouth unwillingly opened. Her great-grandfather had bribed Bernard's way into power? "I tried my hardest, dear girl." Bernard gently cupped Olivia's cheek. "I tried to do good. But you must understand that the only thing that matters in London is money, and what you are willing to do with it. A gentleman will make a generous donation and a law will not pass. A lord will buy an MP votes and the costs of living stays up. It was a sad state of affairs. I did not stand for my seat in the next election." Bernard smiled, his blue eyes warming. "Instead I returned to Derbyshire. I married my beloved Jane, and I devoted myself to my family, to being a father to Colin and Lorna."

As much as her mother did not understand or accept Olivia's ambitions in life, Olivia had to believe that part of Ruth's character had to be attributed to these events that had occurred throughout her childhood. Why was Ruth not mentioned in Bernard's efforts to be a more devoted father?

"And grandfather," Bernard added, smiling at Olivia. "I pride myself on being a good grandfather to my sweet Olivia, too. You are always such a good girl."

Olivia put on a false smile. She was grateful that Lorna never told Bernard about her actions. She would not want him to change his opinion of her. She valued few opinions of her character. Bernard's was one of them.

Olivia got to her feet and kissed her grandfather on the forehead. "I love you, Grandpapa. I have to go away for a while, but I will write," she promised. Olivia motioned for Kit to follow her. She noticed Kit looked slightly ashen in his face. She could see his apprehension.

"Enjoy the dance, dear," murmured Bernard as he returned to his newspaper. "Lovely to meet you, Kurt."

"Er, lovely to meet you, too, sir," replied Kit.

Once they were outside, and the door was closed, Kit spoke.

"I don't want to be involved in that corruption, Olivia," he said firmly. "I have a vision, but from what your grandfather said, it sounds as though corruption is inevitable. I thought ... I thought ... people would vote for me because of the kind of life I would be offering them."

"That is where you are naïve, Kit." Lorna joined them outside the sitting room. She had a knowing, yet sympathetic, smile on her face. "Parliament is not divided into Whigs and Tories. Those men, and I am not saying all, but they are there at the pleasure of those who control them. I know if you are intending to take Olivia with you that you share her sense of right and wrong. Those people who would tend to agree with you do not get a vote on election day. Only those whose bank books fit the criteria do. They are the people you need to please. And I am afraid that you will not please them by offering," Lorna shook her head as she tried to think of an example, "schooling for the poor until they are of age. The poor are their workers. If they are in school, then they cannot work. Do you understand me?"

Olivia's heart instantly fell. How had she not thought of that? Had she really been so swept up in the idea of Kit, the People's Man, winning his way into parliament promising education and an equal chance? Yes, yes, she had.

But the idea of rejection was frightening. Rejection was a wound that would never quite heal. It would fester, and then scab, and then something would happen to make it bleed all over again.

What if the people did not like Kit? What if the people rejected her?

"But what if they were compensated?" proposed Kit. "They cannot have young workers, so they may be compensated for proven claims of additional wages needed to pay adults. The government would be repaid in the taxes earned by a person with a better education in the end, anyway."

Lorna's eyebrows rose. "Well, I stand corrected. Now you are thinking like a politician."

"I won't be controlled, Miss Murray," Kit said adamantly. "I won't be elected at the behest of a benefactor who wishes to influence my decisions. I want to make a difference to the lives of the underprivileged, and perhaps that may be a naïve goal for and MP, but I have to try."

Perhaps Olivia had a lot to learn, too. It seemed, in order to get her way, she would have to learn the art of compromise. She smiled proudly at Kit. He seemed to have the hang of it already. They would teach each other.

As he spoke to Lorna, Kit had such a look of determination on his face. Olivia decided there was nothing more attractive in a man ... in a friend, she mentally corrected ... than one who was speaking of his passions.

"Well, then, I wish you luck," said Lorna. Her eyes then went to Olivia. They softened as he bottom lip trembled. "Olivia..."

Olivia went to her aunt and hugged her tightly. "It is not goodbye forever, Aunt Lorna," she promised. "I will come back," Her eyes flicked to Kit who was watching their embrace, "with a newly elected MP, God willing."

"I still think that you ought to have a chaperone, but nothing I ever say seems to change your stubborn mind," Lorna said as she pulled away. "I pray you will not lose your sense of justice, Olivia. It is a very fine part of your character," she praised. "Possibly my favourite, thought it may turn my hair grey."

Olivia felt her cheeks warming. "I won't," she promised. Olivia's sense of justice flowed through her veins, as though it kept her alive.

"I am entrusting her to you, Kit," Lorna's tone changed to that of a warning. "You must let no harm come to her."

"I am sure it will be quite the other way around, Miss Murray. Olivia will be the one keeping me out of harm's way," Kit offered jokingly, quickly sensing Lorna's seriousness. "I promise. We will keep each other safe."

"I know you may not want to, but perhaps you ought to write to your mother," Lorna suggested quietly. "Ruth would want to know if you were leaving this house. This is where she sent you, after all."

Olivia sucked in a harsh breath. "Banished more like," she muttered. Olivia could feel her scab, the one that had partially healed, with her aunt's words picking at it, willing it to bleed. "No, Mama would not care one way or the other," Olivia decided.

Lorna looked at Olivia sadly. "If she writes me, then I must tell her."

Olivia sighed. The wound was bleeding again. "Seeing as she has not uttered a word since I arrived here then I find that highly unlikely." It seemed ridiculous, really. Olivia had never felt overwhelming maternal love from Ruth. She had never felt lukewarm love from Ruth. How could this affect her so, and after all this time?

"Well, you both ought to get some rest. You have quite the journey ahead of your tomorrow." Lorna offered Olivia one last sympathetic glance before moving on down the hallway.

Olivia then dared to look up at Kit after that display. She could tell that Kit wanted to ask her if she was alright, but was not sure if it was his place.

"I told you I would tell you about it in Hertfordshire," she reminded him, "after your win."

Kit accepted that with a nod. "You are still so certain we can do this?"

Olivia nodded. "Absolutely. My belief has never wavered, just my initial thoughts on how simple this would be. But Aunt Lorna believes you have a head for politics, and so do I."

Kit grinned. "Now we have to convince everyone else."

Chapter 12

Kit did not sleep well at all. The argument he had with his father kept filling his mind. He still felt such anger towards his father, at the same time feeling guilt as he was the son and was therefore meant to concede.

Kit could not concede though. In doing so he would simply be falling into his old habits. Instead, Kit filled his mind with thoughts of the journey ahead.

It would not be easy. It would be difficult and morally compromising; Bernard Murray's insight had proven that. Kit would not only need to appeal to the everyman, but to the wealthy, the prejudiced, and the gentry as well.

Kit would need to find a way to please everyone, which was universally acknowledged to be an impossible task.

Those thoughts were what kept him up for the rest of the night.

Was he taking on too much? Was he too ambitious? Who was he to challenge and champion such reform? He was nobody of consequence.

Certainly, Kit had gained a little fame over the summer having prevented the prince's assassination, but that did not mean that he was experienced enough to sit in parliament.

Olivia believed that he could secure the vote. She had such blind faith that her vision of the world would come to fruition. What if he disappointed her as well? Kit did not think he could take disappointing his father and Olivia. That was altogether too much.

But what if he could not find his words when it truly mattered? What if, when the moment came, Kit did not know what to say? Panic filled Kit's body at the thought of being seen as stupid by others.

That feeling, to Kit, was simply unacceptable. He had spent his first fourteen years of life feeling stupid. Kit remembered feeling such worthlessness at the point in his life. He was stupid, and not worth wanting. But in learning to read, in having a man in a far superior position take a chance on him, Kit had found his worth. He had found his confidence, and he had made something of himself.

Granted, being a university educated factory owner was not his goal, Kit had still achieved it. A chance was all he needed. That was all anyone needed.

Kit exhaled as he settled into his pillow. The panic seemed to pass as he renewed his sense of purpose in his mission. Kit was entering parliament to give those who would not normally see the helping hand of an MP a chance.

Kit fell asleep imagining the look of pride in Olivia's eyes if he managed to get himself elected. He would make her proud. His father, too.

"Wake up!"

Kit woke with a start to see a frenzy of red curls brushing over his face as his bedclothes were pulled back.

"Get up, get up!" Olivia said excitedly. "Come on, the carriage is downstairs. Our cook has packed us breakfast. Get dressed."

Kit sat up with a start to see that Olivia was fully dressed as she began to gather the few possessions that Kit had brought with him. Her blue gown appeared sturdy and practical, and she was already adorned with a brown travelling cloak. Her red hair was loose and wavy down her back.

Kit liked her hair like that.

He then suddenly realised he was in rather an embarrassing state of undress. "Olivia!" he hissed. "I am not wearing any trousers!" Kit's nightshirt barely covered his thighs.

Olivia's blue eyes flicked to his legs, and she giggled, her cheeks flushing. "Well, er, you go on and get dressed then, and I shall wait downstairs."

Kit was quite conscious of the fact that his height made his legs appear rather thin. They were not the muscled tree trunks that women's romance books described the ideal man having. They were not the most attractive part of his anatomy, and for Olivia's first time in seeing him in any state of undress, he would have preferred her to see something that looked less like stilts. Next time he would try to be a little more impressive.

Kit stopped himself. Next time? "Good God, man," he chided himself. "Have a little more respect." Olivia was trusting Kit with her reputation. He could not be imagining the two of them in compromising situations.

No matter how pretty and lovely her hair looked this morning.

Kit had nearly kissed her once already. He could not let what happened in his father's study happen again. Besides that one moment of vulnerability, she had given no indication of affection for him. Kit could not betray her trust in him.

Not unless she gave him permission. Kit sighed as he pulled on his trousers and found his boots and coat. He was human after all.

As Olivia said goodbye to her aunt, and promised to write, Kit felt another sting of guilt. He had almost expected his mother to appear on the Murray's doorstep and beg him to come home. But she did not. Kit expected Cassian was still too angry to let Faith leave. Kit knew he would need to make amends with his parents someday, but it would not be until he had something to show his father.

"You look after her," Lorna said in a warning tone to Kit, once Olivia was already inside the carriage. "This is not a joke to her. She could get hurt."

Kit took heed of Lorna's warning. "I do not intend to disappoint her."

Lorna's brown eyes softened. "I am sure you won't. But Olivia has big dreams, too. Don't forget that."

Kit nodded. Olivia's dreams were to see change. In being elected, he could not disappoint her.

"It feels real now, doesn't it?" Olivia said excitedly as the carriage pulled away from the house.

"Are you ready?" asked Kit.

Olivia grinned. She held up a well-loved copy of Declaration of the Rights of Woman and of the Female Citizen. "Olympe and I have been ready for years, Kit."

As the hours went on, Kit and Olivia began to discuss his goals for the election. Of course, it would first be prudent to get to know the people he would be representing. Then he could present them with his plans for the future.

There was a reason so many of the poor could not read or write, and that was simply because they needed to work to feed their families. Education was secondary.

"It is a vicious cycle," remarked Kit. "They need to work, and their children to work, and so their education is sacrificed, but a higher paying occupation is a possibility when literate."

"The compensatory idea that you came up with yesterday was brilliant," replied Olivia. "If wages were higher, children would not need to work, and they could be in school longer."

Olivia produced a slate from her satchel, just like the sort they had in schoolrooms. Kit almost asked where she had procured it, but she began to write sums. "The war tax," Olivia began, "takes money from each person's income to fund the British effort against Napoleon. The poor, as they stand, are taxed little to none based on their pathetic income. Right now the government receives nothing from these people. But if funding were given to their masters to increase wages so that their children could attain higher qualifications, just imagine the thousands, no, the millions of people that could be taxed for the government's benefit. The revenue would appease anyone."

Kit could practically see Olivia's brain racing. "You know that is not a popular method," he reminded her. The rich did not like handing over anything from their yearly income.

"I know," Olivia huffed, "but these people speak the language of pounds, shillings, and pence. Imagine this. Your father has, what, five hundred workers?"

"Thereabouts."

"Let us pretend that each worker has three children, just an estimation," continued Olivia. "That is fifteen hundred children. If each of them are able to improve themselves through education and attain a job earning, say, two hundred pounds a year. Ten percent of that will be taken in tax. That is twenty pounds for each of those fifteen hundred children. That would ..." Olivia began scrawling away on the slate, "thirty thousand pounds from your father's worker's alone!"

Kit was speechless at Olivia's quick arithmetic. With just an idea, she had raised thirty thousand pounds. No matter the ill feeling towards taxes, when it was not coming out of their own pockets, the rich could not deny that the possibility of such revenue was exciting, and it was a potential way to move forward with their plans.

Olivia seemed to notice Kit's silence. "Oh, well, it is just an idea."

"A brilliant one," remarked Kit, finding his tongue.

Blood filled Olivia's cheeks once again and she turned away from him bashfully. "I understand now, better than I did, about how we need to give something for everything we take."

"What are we going to take?"

Fourteen was minimum age for boys to leave school, Kit and Olivia decided. At that age, they would be able to seek work, an apprenticeship, or continue on with their studies. For girls, it was sixteen.

"Perhaps a college should be established. We could seek private donations, and make it free of charge for those who cannot afford to seek study at more expensive institutions," Kit mused. "Girls especially could attend, and learn to be writers, or poets, or teachers. Whatever they want."

Kit's thoughts wandered to his younger sister, Lucy. While she was privileged financially, it was highly unlikely that she would be successful in the same circles that Emma would be. Perhaps a college like that would be beneficial to her as well. She could pursue anything she wanted.

"A college?" Olivia repeated softly, snapping Kit out of his daydream.

"Bad idea?"

"No!" cried Olivia, shaking her head vehemently. "It is my favourite one yet," she said proudly. In her excitement, she had moved closer to Kit, their legs now touching through the fabric of their clothing. Olivia's cheeks were nearly as red as her hair as she looked at him, her blue eyes betraying her nerves.

For a moment Kit saw that vulnerability he had seen in his father's study. Olivia rarely gave anything away, but he could see it. He had only made that promise not to compromise her mere hours ago, but she was making it increasingly more difficult by the second.

Olivia was so powerful and intelligent, which only increased her effortless beauty. The mysteriously vulnerability that she tried so hard to conceal only increased Kit's interest.

Kit was staring at her. He had not blinked, knowing this because of the dryness he now felt in his eyes, but he did not want to look away. What was she going to do?

Instead of moving even closer to him, as Kit had willed her to do, Olivia moved away. She exhaled a breath she had been holding, looked down and her lap and said, "Being a wife and a mother should not be the only path in life for a woman. There should be choices. There should be opportunity. That is what I want."

Chapter 13

The county seat in Hertfordshire was currently held by Whig politician, Lawrence Powell. From what Olivia had discovered in her brief research of Powell himself, and the seat, Powell looked after the interests of the rich men who supported him, such as merchants and bankers.

Powell did not support reform in voting, and instead relied on those with financial means to keep him in power.

It would be difficult to persuade Powell's supporters to endorse Kit instead. They had an easy parliamentary vote on their interests with Powell. Kit, however, would not be a conformist.

The Tories, however, were eager for a win. Olivia believed that the Tories thought Powell weak in comparison to some of his other Whig colleagues, and as such, vulnerable to losing his seat. Powell was noted for having a few scandals attached to his name, mostly involving women that were not his wife. Of course they had been hushed away, but discretion in the first place would have solved the problem of a tarnished reputation.

Staying faithful to his wife in the first place could have also helped the situation.

Olivia was confident that if Kit could look after the interests of these rich men, he could achieve real change.

Perhaps it was premature, but Olivia had already written ahead of Kit's candidacy. Of course she had not received a reply as they were so soon departing, but Kit was an excellent choice in candidate.

He was highly educated. He was the son of a respected businessman. He had also been knighted by the King over the summer. Olivia hoped that Kit's reputation would be enough to secure more votes purely so that he did not have to bargain with leeches.

As the carriage moved into the city of Hertford, Olivia knew they were in the heart of the seat that Kit would be contesting. He would convince these people to put in him power. He would be the beginning of change, and Olivia would be right alongside him.

She could feel the nerves in her stomach flutter and the reality startled to settle in. This was it. Everything she had ever hoped to see come to fruition would start today.

Olivia stole a glance at Kit, whose eyes were fixed on his window as she watched the city go by. Olivia felt so attached to Kit already, which was a very confusing feeling. Olivia had effectively handed Kit all of her hopes and dreams, and to potentially fail again was heartbreaking. But she felt as though the attachment was quickly growing into something more daunting. Neither her mother nor Aunt Lorna had ever explained things to her properly, but Olivia knew what it was to find a man attractive.

She had known it eight years ago when she had given Kit her very first kiss.

What was even more frightening to Olivia was the fact that she felt that desire resurfacing, and there was only one direction in which they could go if she gave into that desire.

Wife. Mother.

Olivia wanted so much more than that. Her life was not meant to be like every other girl's. If it was, then she would not have been born with the spirit that she had. She was meant to be a champion, not a politician's wife.

Kit turned towards her suddenly, his excited green eyes catching her staring at the back of his head. "What do we do now?" he asked her.

"We get to know the people. Your people," replied Olivia.

It was not long after Kit and Olivia's arrival in Hertford that the Tories did announce Kit as their candidate for the next election. Kit's reputation spared him from needing to meet with the senior parliamentary members. They did not have to know of his true ambitions ... yet.

The flurry of interest in Kit was suddenly extraordinary, but Kit handled it beautifully.

He did exactly as Olivia said. He got to know the people. In order to drum up popular opinion of his character, and therefore to interest those who were financially able to vote in the election, Kit canvassed by visiting the churches, schools, and hospitals. He listened to their concerns, and often proposed careful solutions.

Kit needed to be clever. He needed to listen to and support these people, but he could not promise them the world in a way that would discourage the rich from pursuing him as their MP.

Olivia hated that part. But she understood the rules.

Olivia did her best to help him in this endeavour. She spoke highly of her friend, and informed everyone who would listen of Kit's fine, fair character. But the question she received most often vexed her.

"Are you Mr Kensington's wife?"

"No," she always replied, "I am Mr Kensington's political advisor." To which Olivia received smirks, grimaces, and looks of utter confusion.

Nevertheless, Kit's popularity was immense, and it grew by the day. They had only been canvassing in Hertford a fortnight before Kit was invited to dinner by Mr Frank Hadley, the wealthiest banker in the county.

Olivia had not been expressly invited, and had not intended to go. She did not want the rudeness of arriving uninvited to take away from the importance of the evening for Kit. But Kit has insisted that she accompany him, and had written to Mr Hadley expressly requesting an invitation for his political advisor as well.

Olivia could not pretend that she was not terribly flattered that Kit referred to her as such as well.

Olivia dressed in the best gown that she had brought with her. It was red, and perhaps too dramatic a colour for dinner, but her mother had picked the fabric a few years ago when she still cared about Olivia's affairs. Olivia liked it nonetheless. Olivia wore only a golden cross around her neck and a red ribbon in her hair as her accessories.

Once she was ready, she sat down at the writing desk in the little hotel in which they were staying. Her room was small, but comfortable. Kit was staying in the room next door.

Olivia looked over herself once more in the mirror. Perhaps her choice in dress was a little too theatrical. These were serious, conservative men that she was to converse with this evening. Olivia ran her fingers over the soft, linen skirt and grabbed a fist full of the material in her hand.

She could almost hear her mother telling her she was ridiculous.

"What I wear is of no consequence," decided Olivia. "It should be what I have to say that is important."

While she waited for Kit to collect her, Olivia opened the letter that had arrived from her aunt while they had been out canvassing that day.

It read:

Dearest Olivia,

I was so glad to receive your letter, and to hear that you were well and had found somewhere safe to stay. Papa is glad, too. I explained it as best I could. I believe he thinks you are downstairs, the poor dear.

I hope you are finding Hertfordshire to your liking. I hope the people are receptive and the outcome is favourable. Might I again remind you not to don male clothing and vote in the election yourself. Hertfordshire is a little far for me to travel to pay for your bail. Perhaps if you plan on doing anything reckless you might allow me to speak to Mr Kelly about it first.

Olivia stopped. She wondered if her aunt was wanting an excuse to talk to the charming magistrate who had so rattled her in their first meeting. Olivia continued.

Mrs Kensington came to visit me today. She calls herself Faith now, but I did know her as Anne all those years ago. She wanted to know if I had received any news from the two of you. Could you please ask Kit to write to his poor mother? Whatever happened between him and his parents, he owes them news of his safety. She looked so heartbroken, the poor lady, and in her condition, too! I would wager she has not two full months before the child comes.

Olivia had not the heart to ask Kit over the last two weeks if he had written to his family. He had not mentioned them, and Olivia knew it would be a topic of soreness if she were to bring it up. But thinking of her aunt so sad, and so far along with her child, Olivia knew it was the right thing to do.

We love you and miss you, dear girl. We think of you often, but never have to wonder what you are up to. You are off changing the world. I am proud, no matter how you vex me at times.

Be safe.

All my love,

Lorna

Olivia folded her aunt's letter and put it away. She would reply in the morning. She and Kit needed to get through this evening successfully, and then she would broach the subject of him writing to his own family.

Just as she stood up from the desk, there was a soft rap on the door. Olivia rose from her chair and answered it. Kit was standing there, straining his eyes to look down at his untidy cravat.

"I don't know what is wrong with this bloody thing," he cursed, "but it will not tie correctly."

Olivia immediately saw the problem. Kit was nervous. "Your hands are shaking. Let me." Olivia brushed Kit's hands away, which led to him looking away from his cravat and at Olivia.

Kit's green eyes immediately widened. "You ..." he gasped.

Olivia stepped away bashfully. Perhaps she really ought to change. She had been called a devil child a dozen times. Perhaps wearing red would only encourage such thoughts. "My mother ordered it several years ago ... said it went with my hair ... I don't know. What do you think?"

Kit cleared his throat and managed to compose himself. "I think you look perfect," he said sincerely.

Olivia felt her cheeks turn the colour of her dress. "Let me sort that cravat out," she said, changing the subject. She had lots of experience fixing cravats. Her grandfather needed the help as his fingers were not as nimble as they once were. She quickly tied it at his collar and stepped backward to admire her work. "Now you are perfect, too."

Kit did look very dashing. Like Olivia, he had adorned his best suit. Of course, he had barely brought anything with him from Derbyshire, and so his best suit needed to be purchased. His breeches were far too short, owing to his height, but they were carefully concealed inside his newly polished boots.

"Shall we?" Kit offered Olivia his arm.

She nodded, and accepted it, and together, they left her room.

The journey to Mr Frank Hadley's home was short. He lived in close proximity to the city, and to his bank. His house was the finest townhouse on Dudley Street, and several carriages were stationed outside. This was to be quite the affair.

Olivia could see that Kit's hands were shaking again. She immediately took his hand to calm him as they stepped out onto the street. "You only need to do what you have been doing this past fortnight. Making these people trust you."

"Only?" Kit replied sarcastically. "I don't want to be a puppet, Olivia."

"Then don't be!" she retorted. "You are open to negotiation, but you have your own principles. We have practiced this," she reminded him. "I will not leave your side," she promised.

Olivia felt Kit hold onto her hand even tighter. "Good. Don't."

Chapter 14

The Hadley's door was opened by a smartly dressed servant who took their coats. Kit and Olivia were then led into the Hadley's dining room, their company having already arrived and taken their seats.

The men all rose as soon as Kit and Olivia entered. Olivia saw that the Mr and Mrs Hadley were joined by two other couples. She recognised Mr Roger West. He, like Mr Hadley, was one of the wealthiest men in Hertford. As a landed gentleman, he made his fortune from dozens of rents, and held a position of power over the greater population.

The other couple was one that Olivia had not been expecting to see. Lawrence Powell had joined them for dinner. Of course the sitting member was present. These men wanted to compare their options. Their current puppet, or Kit.

Olivia began to realise that this dinner was a lot more important than they had originally thought.

"Sir Christopher Kensington and Miss Olivia Pendleton," introduced the servant.

Olivia put a smile on her face, hoping to mask her nerves. She stole a glance up at Kit and saw that he was doing something similar.

"Kensington," greeted Mr Hadley, "so good of you to join us this evening." He beckoned Kit and Olivia in, though Olivia noticed that he did not acknowledge her presence. Mr Hadley gestured to a chair for Kit, while Olivia was guided to a chair on the opposite side of the round table, sitting in between two of the wives.

Kit's eyes flashed to Olivia's, as he regretfully watched her be removed from his side. What annoyed Olivia most was that a large floral centrepiece was blocking her view of the men opposite her. It was as though the arrangement was specifically placed there to keep her out of the conversation.

Olivia knew that she needed to make the best of this evening for Kit. If she could not partake in the men's conversation, then she needed to use the influence that these women had over their husbands.

"Hello," she greeted nervously.

Two ladies were seated to her left, while the last was on her right. The lady on her right had red hair, like Olivia, but it was perhaps a little more golden. Olivia liked the colour. She was very pretty, but her fine bone structure, combined with a disapproving expression on her face, made her seem very severe.

"Lovely to make your acquaintance, Miss Pendleton. I am Mrs Virginia Hadley," she introduced herself. "Next to you is Mrs Margaret West, and Mrs Nancy Powell."

"It is a pleasure," said Olivia.

"What are your thoughts on the bill, Kensington?" Olivia heard Mr Hadley ask Kit. "Powell here has some interesting opinions. I would like to know what you think."

What bill were they talking about? Olivia craned her neck but she could not see them from around the irritating foliage.

"Your dress is ... very pretty," Margaret West complimented half-heartedly, taking Olivia's attention away from the men's conversation. Margaret was also an attractive woman, perhaps around her Aunt Faith's age. Though her skirt concealed it well, Olivia could tell that Margaret was with child.

"Thank you," murmured Olivia. "My mother had it made for me a few years ago."

"Oh yes, we could tell by the sleeves," interjected Nancy Powell. Nancy looked the most bitter of the three women. Her hair was light blonde, and her eyes were a cold blue. The lines on her face told Olivia that she scowled a lot, and with good reason knowing her husband's reputation.

Olivia frowned. These ladies did not approve of her. It was not a foreign phenomenon, and it did not hurt her feelings. It took a lot more than a nasty comment to hurt Olivia. Ordinarily she would ignore it, or make a nasty comment back. It was common knowledge that Nancy's husband kept other women, but Olivia could not stoop to that level. She needed these women on her side.

Olivia quickly searched Nancy's person to find something to compliment. She gasped. "But that brooch is divine," she lauded. "Wherever did you get it?"

Nancy was taken aback, and placed her hand over the sapphire brooch she wore on her gown. "It was my mother's, thank you."

"Now that we mention parents, yours are the Earl and Countess of Runthorpe, is that correct?" asked Virginia.

Olivia's parents were a soft subject for her. She nodded. "Yes, they are," she confirmed. "Though I am not sure they wish to be associated with me." There was no point lying to these women.

"I would imagine not," agreed Margaret, "knowing that their daughter is a glorified mistress."

Olivia recoiled and stared at Margaret West. "I beg your pardon, Mrs West?"

"Come now," said Virginia. "No one believes this nonsense of you being Sir Christopher's political advisor! What a joke!" she laughed lightly.

"What is so funny about it?" Olivia demanded to know.

At that moment the servants began to set the first course in front of them. Olivia waited for the vegetable soup to be ladled before continuing.

"Why shouldn't Kit seek advice from me?"

Margaret frowned. "Men do not take advice from women, dear," she said with pity. "If that is what he is telling you in order to make you feel as though you are not merely his mistress then I am afraid you are terribly naïve."

"Mrs West, I have been called many things, many things that are entirely true, but I am not Kit's mistress. I would never lower myself in that way. I am a woman with a brain in my head and a voice in my lungs and I have found a friend, a man, who will listen to me. It has taken a long time for someone to listen to me, but Kit does. I am helping him to become the sort of MP who votes for the benefit of the people, advocates for them, and enacts change that creates a better society then there was before."

"But Miss Pendleton, the world does not work like that," Virginia said critically. "The only thing that matters is money, and how much and how quickly one can make it. No amount of schoolgirl idealisms is going to change the way men think. You might think that Sir Christopher listens to you, but I would wager his mind is somewhere far more scandalous," she whispered.

Nancy and Margaret nodded in agreement. It seemed they did not think very much of Kit either, or they were simply used to less than agreeable men. It then occurred to Olivia that these women, just as she was, were blocked from the conversation on the other side of the table.

They were excluded, too. They felt as though their opinions were unwanted because they were.

"Does is bother you when your husband's neglect to solicit your advice on a decision?" Olivia pondered to the group. "Does is bother you that we can be speaking of them as we are and they have no idea, and yet were are sitting mere feet from them?"

"But at what price?" Mr West demanded to know, proving Olivia's point. What they were discussing, Olivia did not know, because she had not been included in the conversation.

Virginia, Margaret, and Nancy seemed to be seriously considering Olivia's question. All four bowls of soup were practically aban- doned.

"It bothers me," continued Olivia. "It bothers me that I am consid- ered less intelligent purely because of the fact that I wear a skirt. It bothers me that men with less intelligence than a drawing pin can sit in university lecture halls while the best education that I could hope to receive would centre on the proper way to curtsey. It bothers me that there are people of great integrity who lack opportunity purely based on their income." Olivia looked Virginia Hadley right in the eye and said, "It bothers me that you would assume first that I was

Kit's mistress because no woman could advise a man on politics. Does it bother you?" she asked again.

The three women exchanged glances of knowing. Olivia was unsure if that was a good or bad thing.

"Well, Miss Pendleton," said Virginia, "I no longer believe you are Sir Christopher's mistress." She picked up her soup spoon and began to eat.

Olivia frowned. "What do you believe then?"

"You are the type of woman who would scare many men," said Margaret.

"You scare my husband. You and your candidate," added Nancy.

Olivia tried her hardest to not smile triumphantly. Lawrence Powell was scared of them?

"I still think you are naïve, Miss Pendleton, very naïve. Tonight will be the first of many where you will find yourself cut off from the conversation, but if a woman like you can respect a politician, then perhaps he is decent," Virginia decided.

Olivia was glad to have what seemed like the gradual respect of these ladies, but she was determined to never be cut off from the conversation like this again.

The conversation shifted to the upcoming winter parties as the meat course was brought out. Olivia tried her best to listen to what was happening on the other side of the table. From what she could make out, Kit was doing well. He was speaking confidently about reform, while answering the concerns of Mr Hadley and Mr West with consideration.

Lawrence Powell seemed to be growing considerably more frustrated. Olivia could hear his panicked comments and retorts, but she had not been expecting what he said next.

"You know his mother is a whore, don't you?" he announced loudly.

All conversation, even between the ladies, stopped. The sound of cutlery hitting plates and drinking glasses being abandoned followed.

Olivia gasped in shock. Nancy paled in response to her husband's thoughtless attack.

"What did you just say?"

Olivia had never heard such fury in Kit's voice, not even when he was arguing with his father. His voice sounded like he was about read to hurl his knife at the MP.

"You all remember the big scandal in the newspapers years ago, about Anne Pendleton returning from the dead. Well, it turned out she was living as a whore with a soldier, and had a bastard child! Anne Pendleton is this man's mother!"

Olivia balled her hands into fists and closed her eyes. She could practically feel the anger that was radiating off of Kit. She could only imagine the shade of red his face was turning.

"Powell, really, that is not dinner conversation," chided Mr Hadley.

"Isn't it?" challenged Mr Powell. "Is his background really the sort we want representing us? The son of a whore, raised alongside a bastard sister. Who knows what he might want to sanction? Perhaps bigamy? Perhaps he wants us all to be like his mother and live in sin. He is already doing so with that girl!"

Olivia could not see him, but she knew Mr Powell was pointing at her.

"Everyone knows she is his whore, just like his mother is his father's whore!"

Kit threw back his chair and stood up from the table. Olivia could now see him over the top of the centrepiece. He was as red and as furious looking as she had predicted. But the ire in his eyes was truly terrifying. "That is enough, sir!" he bellowed. "My mother is the best woman I know. She would quite literally give even you her very last penny if it would help you. She is kind and generous, and has the character and patience of a saint. She has raised my sisters and me to be good people, and so help me God, if you utter another derogatory word in her direction I will challenge you to a duel, don't think I won't." Kit then looked at Olivia. He was still furiously angry. "The same goes for Miss Pendleton. I will not have her reputation tarnished by your disgusting accusations. I say she is my political advisor because that is what she is. I would wager you would not find fifty minds in the House of Commons who are quite as bright or enlightened as she is. I would be a fool not to take advantage of her wisdom. If you would have taken the time this evening to get to know her, instead of judging her, you might have realised just why I value her as I do. John 8:7 says 'He that is without sin among you, let him cast the first stone'. Can you honestly tell me, sir, that you are in a position to be saying such accusations?"

Lawrence Powell had no response. He had too much pride to apologise, and not enough courage to counter argue. Instead he announced that he and Nancy would be leaving immediately.

The last thing Nancy said before leaving the table was, "I hope you win," under her breath.

"Simpkins, take this display away, I cannot see my guests," ordered Mr Hadley as soon as the Powells were away.

The servant removed the floral arrangement and the table was suddenly open. The ladies were involved in the conversation for the rest of the meal, however the conversation remained light after Lawrence Powell's display.

But from the way Mr Hadley and Mr West were looking at Kit, Olivia could tell that he had won their respect.

"I do not think you comprehend the level of influence you have over young Mr Kensington, Miss Pendleton," remarked Mr Hadley to Olivia quietly as the guests were saying their farewells. "He has a wonderful moral compass, but I would wager good money that if you asked him to jump, he would leap up onto the dining room table. A man so easily manipulated is very intriguing to me."

Olivia merely arched an eyebrow and decided to say nothing. Let him think that Kit was easy to manipulate. They would learn that he was quite the opposite when he was in power.

Kit's moral compass was stronger than anything.

Chapter 15

They had been in the carriage for near three hours. Kit would have been anxious to stretch his legs and regain feeling in his buttocks were he not so excited to arrive at their destination. He wanted to surprise Olivia. He wanted to thank her.

And, if he were being honest, he wanted to set in motion the notion of courtship. Where on earth was he ever going to meet a girl like Olivia? There were none so intelligent or passionate, and hardly any as pretty as she was.

The idea had never been settled, not really. But how could it not be on both of their minds? It seemed to be on everyone else's. It angered him greatly whenever he heard unkind whispers about Olivia's role within Kit's camp.

Kit was attracted by Olivia's character and countenance, but he would be lying if he said that he was not more so by her appearance. And she looked especially beautiful tonight. She was wearing the same red dress that she had been wearing at the Hadley's the other night. He liked that dress, and thought it suited her well. Red was her colour.

Twice they had nearly kissed and each time Olivia had displayed such hesitation. Kit wanted to quell all thoughts of hesitation and encourage her affection.

"Where on earth are you taking me?" Olivia demanded to know playfully. It was now dark out. She could not tell where they were by the appearances of the towns they travelled through.

"You shall see," he replied coyly. "I wrote to my mother today," he informed her, knowing the subject would distract Olivia.

It succeeded. Olivia's eyes widened and warmed as she smiled with pride. "You did?"

Olivia had informed him after having left the Hadley's that her Aunt Lorna had included news of his mother in her letter. Kit had immediately felt a pang of guilt for having left her without even word of his safe arrival in Hertford.

No matter his quarrel with his father, Kit owed his dear mother a letter. Having just defended her honour in the Hadley's dining room, Kit was fresh with regard for her and sat down to pen a letter to her earlier that afternoon.

Kit had been quite at a loss at what to say to her except for that he was safe and well, and that he thought of them often. It was the truth. Kit often thought of his family. He missed his sisters dearly. After having been away at Cambridge for so long, spending merely the summer with them had not been enough to satisfy his need to spend time with them. Kit even missed his father. Of course Kit missed Cassian, but he could not bring himself to ask after him. He could only pray that his father had recovered well from his surgery and was back working.

After all, Cassian has not been the one to inquire after him. Father and son were both as stubborn as the other.

"I forget how our mother's worry," he said thoughtlessly.

Olivia's face dropped ever so slightly, and Kit knew immediately that he had said the wrong thing. She had said once that she would tell him of her mother in time. He hoped tonight would be the night.

Olivia quickly composed herself, and returned to playfully questioning him about their destination.

The lights of London soon betrayed him. The carriage took them to the eastern end of the Strand, to the Groves Restaurant. Kit was not one for fine dining, but he was told that for a guinea, one could receive one of the best meals in London at this establishment.

Olivia looked out the window in shock. She then turned around and asked, "Are we eating here?"

"Yes," confirmed Kit.

"But ... it is so ..." Kit could tell that Olivia did not want to utter the word expensive. Perhaps she thought it rude to question the amount money in his purse.

"Do not worry," he assured her. Kit did not have expensive tastes. He had not spent any money aside from food and board whilst in Hertford. He could afford to take Olivia out for a fine dinner.

They exited the carriage and were welcomed by the restaurant staff. Their coats were taken and the maître d' seated them at a fine, yet secluded, table in the corner of the restaurant. The restaurant was not large, but it was fine, with twenty or so tables all set out elegantly. The restaurant was about half filled with couples and parties all sitting down to eat delicious smelling food. A string quartet played soft music in the far corner of the room.

Their table was laid out with a white cloth, crystal glassware, with fine white china and silverware. Kit beat the maître d' to pulling out Olivia's chair. Kit obliged him their napkins. A waiter soon attending them with champagne, before he recited them their menu for the evening.

"Good evening, sir, madam," he greeted. "Tonight you will enjoy a cream of artichoke soup to start, followed by a sirloin beef served with carrots, a spectacular chicken fricassee, new potatoes, bread and cream butter, and you will finish with a Madeira cake with refreshment."

Kit had not had such a meal ... ever. Faith always ensured that they ate well at home, but she managed the kitchen with economy, and never over-ordered on meat.

"Excellent," murmured Kit casually, containing his excitement. The waiter departed and Kit raised his glass to Olivia. "I wanted to thank you for everything you have done for me these past weeks, Olivia," Kit said gratefully. "I would not be here without you. Your kindness, your sense, and your belief in me has utterly changed my life for the better."

Olivia's cheeks warmed as she clinked her glass with Kit's. "You did not have to buy me such a fancy dinner in order to thank me, you know," she informed him.

Kit feigned shock as he tasted his champagne. "Oh, you thought that I was footing the bill?"

Olivia rolled her eyes. "Do not tease me. I will wash dishes in the kitchen if it means I get to enjoy such a menu."

"So would I," replied Kit in agreeance. "I am sorry about before," said Kit, deciding to address his gaff in the carriage. "What I said about mothers. It was careless." He was not so altruistically encouraging Olivia to confide him.

Olivia took another sip from her champagne glass. "No, do not be sorry." She sighed. "I suppose my experience with my mother has left me rather ... raw." Olivia smoothed out the napkin on her lap as she took a deep breath. "You knew me as a child. I was not so different than I am now, but I was not an easy child."

Kit very well recalled their one meeting as children.

"I was all my parents had. My mother could not have any more children. I was ... am their only child. My mother devoted herself to bringing me up the way she thought I should be, and I resented her terribly for it. I hated etiquette lessons. I did not see the sense in learning French or Latin, and what use did I have for needlework? I saw it as my mother bringing me up to be like her, and when I looked at my mother, she was the epitome of what I did not want to be."

At that moment, their waiter returned with their soup and placed the bowls in front of them, however, Kit was too engrossed in Olivia's story to eat.

"My father is a clergyman, and I think he always resented me for not being a son. This only fuelled my determination to not be a perfect little girl. I was not allowed to read popular books, so they were exactly what I sought out to find. And it was after procuring Declaration of the Rights of Woman and of the Female Citizen that I started to understand the true divide between myself and those classed lower than I was." Olivia lifted her soup spoon to her mouth and made a sound of satisfaction. "This is really excellent, you should eat," she encouraged.

"I will," he promised. "Go on," he prompted.

"I would do things like give away my possessions to people who needed them more than I did," continued Olivia. "It infuriated my mother," she recalled. "I would question my father constantly. His sermons were always so harsh. He had an idea of what should be, and I did not agree. I was not allowed to attend church after I openly questioned him during a sermon on a Sunday. I received a thrashing and was forced to pray and read my Bible every Sunday from then on.

"And yet I was not deterred. My education continued, even though I did not care for the subjects. What had I done, save for being born into a privileged family, to deserve such attention to my studies? My village did not even have a school. Children could not educated by illiterate parents. How was it fair? I raided my father's library and paid for a teacher myself, thirty pounds was taken from my dowry to pay her. That was when we met, you recall?

"The world, as I saw it, was not as good as it could be. I endeavoured, and still do, to change it for the better. Of course, my determination to create change only increased, as did my willingness to find myself in trouble. I was arrested more times than I care to admit. My reputation did not matter to me. That was my mother's to worry about. My parents were embarrassed by me and I did not care. They quickly became ashamed of me, and I did not quite understand the effect that would have on me at the time.

"The final straw was when I was fifteen. I had been arrested one too many times for my mother's liking. She no longer cared to collect me from gaols and they subsequently disowned me.

"That is something I do not think we understand as children. We always assume that our parents will always put up with us because we are their children. But sometimes they don't. Mine did not. My parents rejected me, they rejected my very being, everything that I held dear, and it tore a significant hole in my heart. They dismissed me, their only child, and sent me to be my Aunt Lorna's problem. I have not heard from them since."

Olivia spoke with such maturity, yet Kit could hear the level of emotion and sadness that was still in her voice as she spoke of her parents' rejection.

"I have always said that unkind words do not affect me, and that is the truth. I have been called every wicked name under the sun, but rejection is another thing altogether, and rejection by one's own parents is something completely unimaginable. It was as though my very identity was disgusting to them."

Kit could see ghosts in Olivia's blue eyes. To see her so hurt by her parents made him feel frustratingly powerless. How could these people reject their own daughter? Olivia was right. Parents were supposed to love their children, no matter their feelings towards their actions.

Kit immediately thought of his father. Kit knew that he had hurt his father when he had left Derbyshire, but he knew that Cassian loved him. Parents loved their children, even when they did not like them.

"Hang them," said Kit exasperatedly. "Do not let such people haunt you so."

"Don't say that," replied Olivia quietly.

He was taken aback. "Why ever not?" asked Kit.

"Because they are my parents," she replied simply. "They may not be as kind or as loving as your parents, but they are the only parents I have, and no matter how they regard me, there will always be a part of myself that craves their love, and their approval. I suppose I am just a girl in that way. I am a daughter without parents who care about her. I know I am not the easiest person to love, but I do crave that sometimes, to be loved."

Kit was completely bewildered at the conclusion of her speech. She had engaged his attention for a quarter of an hour, detailing the woes of her childhood and the emotional cruelty of her parents, and yet, after all she had endured, all she wanted was to be loved.

But Kit knew they were not the right people to love her. They could not provide her with the type of love she deserved. Kit could do that. In that very moment, Kit made a promise to himself that he would love this woman for as long as she would let him, and in the way that made her feel whole again. And Kit would let Olivia in on this promise just as soon as she was ready to hear it.

Chapter 16

Olivia felt a considerable weight lift off of her shoulders having told Kit about her childhood. She meant every word. She knew she was not the easiest child. She knew that her mother would have adored to have a little girl who liked being measured for dresses, who enjoyed shopping for hats and husbands, and who simply did as she was told.

But that was not who she was, and perhaps naively, she had always presumed her parents would be there. They had never shown her an ounce of support for her interests, nor given her praise or even great affection, but they were still her parents, the only ones she had, and she loved them. Was it really such a high price to ask that they love her too?

Apparently so.

Olivia liked that she had been able to share the pain she had experienced with Kit. She felt as though he understood her properly, and could grasp where her ambitions had come from, and why she behaved the way she did. She was also quietly glad that his feelings towards her had not seemed to change. He still held her in high esteem, and he still watched her and gazed at her with the same admiration that he has since shortly after they had met for the second time ... or perhaps even the first time, when they were children.

Part of Olivia enjoyed his attentions. She adored his attentions. They made her feel accepted for the first time in her life. That feeling was addicting. It drew her to Kit in a way she had never been drawn to anybody in her life.

But the other part of Olivia, the rational, progressive part of Olivia, resisted these attentions. She knew there was only one way in which such attentions could end. Olivia's reputation, not that she cared, but she knew Kit did, was tarnishing by the day. A gentleman like Kit would only allow their expedition to end in one way.

Marriage. Of course, they had not discussed it, and every time their conversations turned remotely towards the subject of feelings Olivia immediately diverted it. Marriage meant being a wife, and Olivia had no desire for such a life.

She only had to look at her mother for an example of what life she did not want. Ruth's concerns centred on her own position in society, her husband's career advancement, ordering around servants, possessing the latest fashions, village gossip, and once, they centred on raising her daughter to be exactly like her.

Olivia had more desire to remove her own toenails then to end up like that.

But still, that feeling of acceptance was addicting, and it almost made her want to forget her objections for a while.

But another feeling started to brew in Olivia's heart in the following weeks. A feeling that was not so kind.

Kit's popularity had reached parliament come November. The weather was changing, but Kit's momentum was only increasing. Lawrence Powell's character attacks were futile at this point. The wealthy were attracted to Kit's ability to negotiate, but the Tories in London were attracted to Kit's youth and energy. So much so that he was starting to receive invitations from powerful people in the party. He was invited to attend dinners, to attend gentleman clubs and smoking parties.

But there was only ever one invitation. Olivia was not welcome. And so an evil feeling started to stew.

Jealousy.

In between invitations, Kit still campaigned as normal. He and Olivia still spent time in Hertford and the surrounding villages, conversing with people who had concerns. Kit toured the schools and the surveyed the working conditions, and Olivia collected the female perspective, and spoke to girls and mothers, all of whom were excited at the possibility of better opportunities at the school.

But this feeling of jealousy was festering, and Olivia hated it. She hated herself for feeling this way, and she felt terribly for Kit who was feeling excited at his potential election in December.

Olivia was not resentful of Kit, only jealous of his ability to find success. For how long had she been shouting such reform from the rooftops? Years! And each time she had somehow found her way to a magistrate's office. In only a short time, Kit had found his way in with the most powerful men in London, shouting the same reform. Olivia was beginning to feel quite powerless, and coupled with her jealousy, it was not a nice constitution to have.

Her smile must have been convincing, as Kit did not seem to notice her internal struggles, nor did she want him to. Olivia did not want Kit to know she was feeling such selfish evils.

"Did you hear?" asked Kit as he sat down to breakfast with Olivia on the morning of December nineteenth. The election was mere days away.

"Hear what?" asked Olivia as she cracked open her boiled egg with the back of her spoon.

"The snow is so bad in the north of the county that the election has been delayed," he remarked in frustration. "They have settled on the tenth of January as the date, to allow the men enough time to clear the snow to allow access to the voting stations." Kit held in his hand a letter that clearly contained the news.

"Oh dear," replied Olivia, setting down her spoon. "Well, I suppose that is the risk they take when they schedule an election in the winter."

Kit nodded. "I ought to organise some relief," he decided. "If the snow is so bad there could be limited access to food and such, especially with Christmas only days away. What do you think?"

Olivia smiled. She knew such kindness would be welcome. Kit was blessed with such a generous heart. It made Olivia hate herself even more for her jealousy. "I think that is a fine idea."

Kit started to share ideas of what he wanted to collect. Olivia listened but her thoughts soon went elsewhere. They had both been away from home for nearly four months. Olivia had been experiencing her hateful emotions for nearly half that time. It was exhausting. Perhaps this delay was a blessing in disguise.

Olivia could not tell Kit about how she was feeling as it was unfair to him, but she could tell her Aunt Lorna. She had not wanted to write about her jealousy to her aunt, as she did not want Lorna to think ill of her, but after nearly eight weeks of exhaustive bitterness, perhaps it was time.

"I think I might go home for Christmas," Olivia announced.

Kit looked at her, astonished. "What?"

"We have been away for nearly four months," continued Olivia. "I think we both ought to go home to see our families now that the election is delayed."

Kit recoiled at the idea. "No, no, I don't think that would be a good idea." Kit had been sporadically communicating with his mother, but he had received no news of his father, and no letter from his father directly. Olivia knew this resistance came from a place of guilt. Kit's emotions were far easier for her to read than it was for him to read her own. "No, I should stay here and render assistance where it is needed. Besides, the snow is terrible. It is not safe to travel."

"I will instruct the driver to go around it," Olivia replied. "I want to see my aunt and my grandfather."

"Olivia, is everything alright?" asked Kit.

Olivia smiled reassuringly, just as she had been all this time to disguise her horrid feelings. "Perfectly," she lied.

Kit seemed to believe her. "You know I care about your wellbeing," he said sincerely. "Very much." Kit reached across the table and took her hand.

Olivia enjoyed the comfort. "I know." Would he still care if he knew how Olivia was really feeling? She looked into his kind, green eyes and saw the genuine regard that he had for her. The feeling of acceptance settled her for a moment, before that overwhelming, envious beast inside of her reared its ugly head.

It was in this moment, and in a few random others, that she wished she was not so ... Olivia-like. How simple it would be to allow herself to love Kit, and to support him in his career. She was certain that Kit would be receptive to that idea. With the way that he was looking at her, she could see the affection and admiration there.

But it could not be. To allow that future would be to deny her very being. The only thing that she could do was try to eliminate this hateful jealousy, and she hoped her aunt would be able to help her with that.

"I want to go home," Olivia said again. "I will return before the election, I promise."

Kit seemed to accept it. "I will organise your travel then," he said, "and instruct the driver to be careful what with the weather."

"What will you do?" she asked.

"I have had several invitations, but I am minded to only accept one. Edward has invited me to the palace for Christmas. He has extended this invitation to you as well, if I can persuade you to stay."

The offer was tempting, but Olivia knew where she needed to be. "No, I cannot. But I am glad he has asked you."

"I have not heard from him at all for the last few months until I received his invitation. I would wager his father was not at all happy on his plans to quit his Cambridge education," mused Kit. His expression changed. "I suppose I can relate to that."

"Would you like to take a message to your family? Even just a few lines?"

Kit smiled and shook his head. "No, I would imagine that would only make my father angrier. I have not heard a word from him in all this time. He has no desire to hear from me."

Olivia could not believe that to be true but she did not press the issue. "I suppose I ought to pack." She stood up from the table and removed her hand from Kit's.

"I will arrange transport for you."

"Thank you," she replied.

As she walked away, Kit called to her, "Olivia!"

Olivia turned.

"I will miss you, you know. I wish you would stay."

"I will miss you, as well," she said sincerely. But how much she had to conceal. She hoped that when she returned she could look upon his successes with pride instead of envy. Kit could not think well of her when she felt as she did, and Olivia wanted Kit to think well of her. Few people thought well of her, after all.

Chapter 17

- -

K it guiltily stuffed his mother's loving wishes of a happy Christmas in the drawer beside his bed. He knew it would have been the right thing to return home and make nice but a significant part of himself just couldn't find the courage to do it.

He supposed he was envious of Olivia in that respect. She was not on bad terms with her family and so she could enjoy the holiday with them.

Kit remained in Hertford, and had elected to journey to London for Christmas instead.

He had spent the time in between travelling organising relief for the families impacted by the snow. Kit had paid for food and ale and hay for the livestock.

But today was the twenty-fifth of December, and it was the first holiday he had spent without his family since they had taken him in. He was lying in what was possibly the most comfortable bed in England in the Palace of William V and was wondering if his sisters likes the dolls and baubles he had sent them.

A royal manservant arrived in his bedroom not long after. Kit was helped into his best suit, his chin was shaved, his hair was combed and his fingernails were cleaned.

"His Royal Highness Prince Edward is waiting for you in the east dining room, sir," the manservant informed Kit once he was ready.

"Thank you," replied Kit as he buttoned his coat. He departed the guest room and ventured out into the corridor.

It was funny now to think that his father's house in Kensington had once seemed like a palace to him. Kit could hardly fathom she sheer size of this building, or the immense cost of each one of the tapestries that adorned the walls.

The sovereign lived here with his three children. The eldest, the Prince of Wales, Edward's elder brother Charles, was the heir to the throne and the favourite son of the monarch, or so Kit was told. Princess Alice was the second, and was equally if not more precious to the King than Charles. Alice was only unmarried because the King could not bear to part with her.

And Edward?

Kit arrived at the east dining room, one of four dining rooms in the palace, and the door was opened for him by a footman.

Edward was slouching on the gold upholstered chairs alone at the round mahogany table, his nose in yesterday's newspaper.

Edward often ate alone and avoided his brother and father as much as he could. There was only so many "I am so disappointed in you, Edward. Why can't you be more like your brother, Charles?" speeches that he could take. And it was a capital crime to strike a sovereign.

"Happy Christmas," greeted Kit. He sat down opposite Edward.

Edward folded the newspaper and set it aside. "Same to you, my friend," he replied and sat up properly. The footmen began to serve the breakfast.

After months on end of eating porridge, it was a real treat to be served pastries, eggs and fruit for breakfast.

"Do you intend to eat at all with your family today?" asked Kit.

Edward's blue eyes narrowed. "Not at all if I can help it. Though I am sure I shall be summoned. My brother cannot think straight if I am not being scolded in front of him. Though I doubt my father would let me out of the royal church tradition."

It was tradition that the royal family attend a church service on Christmas while also giving alms to the poor.

"You will have to remain behind for that. We cannot have our newest MP fraternising with the royals. What would the newspapers say?"

"I am not an MP yet," reminded Kit. "But I agree, it would be unethical."

"What would be unethical?" came a woman's voice as the door to the dining room was opened. Princess Alice entered the dining room, dismissing the servants and seated herself before either Kit or Edward had a chance to stand.

Princess Alice was often considered one of the most beautiful women in Europe. Her portraits that circulated were most accurate. Her eyes were the same shade of blue as Edward's though her hair was darker, almost raven black. Her pale skin was like porcelain and her figure was regarded as most alluring. She was one or two years older than Kit, and was without a doubt the most eligible woman in the world.

Behind closed doors, though, she was kind, witty, and terribly clever. It was no wonder her father favoured her so.

Kit had once fancied himself quite attracted to her, but things had changed. There was a certain redhead who had captured his attention most willingly.

"Kit fraternising with us now that he is soon to be elected," Edward informed Alice.

Alice put on a look of shock. "Oh, dear no. You would not want anyone thinking you receive preferential treatment." Alice laughed. "Silly things forgetting we have not been an absolute monarchy for nearly two centuries." Alice helped herself to a boiled egg and salted it. "We have been reading about you in the newspapers, though, Kit. They paint you in quite an exciting manner. Young blood ready to revolutionise British parliament. I must say, I find it terribly modern of you to have a woman advisor. I commend you."

Kit was glad that some newspapers printed Olivia's role correctly. Those that liked to print gossip used some very un-Christian descriptors. "There was no other choice. If only you could hear Olivia speak, Your Highness. She is a champion for women, and for the lower classes. She is determined to leave the world in a better state than when she entered it. It is an ambition we have come to share."

Alice smiled coyly. "Then I shan't be satisfied until I have heard her speak."

"You shall have the opportunity at their wedding, Alice," teased Edward. "Poor Kit is mad for her, after all."

Kit felt his cheeks warm as Edward grinned.

"Am I wrong? I could see it the minute I saw you two together!"

"Oh, how romantic," remarked Alice.

Edward wasn't wrong at all. This time apart had clarified Kit's decision. He was mad for Olivia. He always had been, ever since she had given him his first kiss as a fourteen year old boy. But he had come to love her as an adult, as a woman, as a person. Kit admired her mind and respected her conviction.

If she would consent to be his, Kit would consider himself to be luckiest man in Britain.

"She is the most remarkable woman I know," said Kit after a while. "I love her, and I don't ever want to be apart from her again. Olivia wants to change the world and I will do my damnedest to help her."

"Cherish her," urged Alice. "The freedom to choose is such a luxury. To have found your soulmate is a rarity."

Kit knew that he was conversing with two people that would have little freedom to make their own choices with regards to matrimony. Edward would be married off just as soon as his father could decide what to do with him, and Alice would be aligned with a European power the minute her father could spare her.

The door to the dining room opened suddenly, and the footman announced, "His Majesty, the King. His Royal Highness, the Prince of Wales."

All three occupants immediately rose to their feet and bowed. Kit did not think he would ever get used to being somewhat acquainted with the royal family. Standing in the presence of the monarch was something that he could never have imagined in wildest dreams as a fourteen year old illiterate orphan.

He did not think the nerves would ever disappear.

The king was a tall, imposing man, with a gruff exterior and an even prickly interior. His expression showed displeasure whenever his eyes seemed to fall on his youngest child.

Edward had once told Kit that his father had resembled a human being when his wife had been alive.

Kit felt an overwhelming pang of guilt in that moment. The king looked at Edward as though he were a burden, an imposition. Kit knew that it made Edward feel terribly.

Kit's own father had never looked at him that way before their argument. There was never a man prouder of his son than Cassian of Kit.

The king was followed by his eldest son, Charles. Charles resembled his father in both looks and expression. Charles was being moulded by the king, and had developed an equal disdain for his younger brother.

Once the king was finished bestowing his cold glare on Edward, his blue eyes turned to Alice. His expression immediately softened. He held true love and tenderness for his daughter.

"I have come to collect your personally, dear Alice," said the king. "I have had a special breakfast prepared in my dining room."

"How kind, Papa," remarked Alice, "but I have already started dining with Edward and our guest, Sir Kit."

The king pursed his lips. "Come now, Alice," he said firmly.

"Do you not want to ask Edward to join us?" asked Alice hopefully. "It is Christmas, after all."

"Come now, Alice." The king would not ask again.

Alice looked to her brother regretfully as she moved away from the table. She followed her father and brother out of the dining room and the door was closed behind them.

"I am sorry, my friend," Kit offered sincerely.

Edward gave him a dismissive shake of the head. "He has barely said a word to me except to scold me since I told him I would not be returning to Cambridge. I just thank God I will never be king. If I were then he would make me shadow him like Charles."

"Could you ever talk to him?"

Edward laughed. "My father would rather cut off his own hand than give me a kind word. He already has a perfect son. What use does he have for me except to marry me off to a foreign princess?"

Kit merely looked down at his plate and found his thoughts wandering to his own father. How they managed to hurt each other and yet how he knew they loved each other. Kit knew he had been a bad son, and he knew that one of these days he would have to stand before his father and utter those exact words.

Chapter 18

Olivia had been home for two days when she awoke on the morning of the twenty-fifth. She had surprised her family, and had immediately been conscripted into helping with their charitable plans.

While Olivia would have much preferred to sit by a fire and pour her heart out to her aunt, taking baskets to families in their village who might not have been having a very merry Christmas was a lovely distraction.

It was still quite early. There was no light peeking in through the drapes and she could not yet hear the maids about the house. Olivia lit her lamp and walked over to her dressing table.

Olivia sat down in front of the mirror and proceeded to brush out her hair. It was knotty from sleeping, suggesting she had tossed and turned quite a bit. As she looked at herself, she could see that she was tired. There were shadows underneath her eyes, and she looked older.

Was this the punishment for jealousy? "Why am I like this?" Olivia asked herself forlornly. Why couldn't she be happy for Kit? Why couldn't she be content with her lot in life? Why was she cursed with such wicked envy?

Olivia thought back to how she was at eleven years old. Kit had found her stealing books from her father's library in order to stock the school room. She was so determined to educate the masses that she resorted to theft. But that was enough. She was helping and it was enough.

Why did it not feel like enough now?

Olivia was doing good on a much larger scale. Kit was more than likely to be elected soon! What good could he accomplish within the halls of Westminster!

And that was where she supposed the jealousy came from. Kit was the one making the achievements that Olivia had always wanted to. She was going to be left out, cast aside, dismissed and talked down to, just because she was a girl.

Olivia buried her head in her hands cursing herself. "Wicked, wicked girl."

"Now, now, that is an unkind word."

Olivia jumped. She had not heard her aunt enter her bedroom. Lorna was dressed only in her nightclothes, her red hair still fixed in rags, and she was carrying her lamp in her hands. Lorna set the lamp down on the dressing table and sat down next to Olivia on the bench seat. She placed a comforting hand on the small of Olivia's back.

"What is the matter, Olivia? You have looked distressed since you arrived."

"I am a terrible person, Aunt Lorna." Olivia promptly let out a loud sob as she revealed that truth.

Lorna hushed her. "That is simply not true," she refuted.

Olivia sniffed. "It is," she persisted. "I am wicked and envious and this horrid feeling has taken up residence in my stomach."

Lorna rubbed Olivia's back. "I don't believe you. Pray, tell me why."

Olivia let out another loud, unladylike sob. Her eyes welled up and she took a minute to compose herself. "All my life, people have told me no. My mother, my father, the law!" she stammered emotionally. "You can't do that, Olivia ... you cannot change things, Olivia ... you are just a girl, Olivia!" Olivia imitated. "I have tried so hard to enact change, to make life just a little bit better for those who are less fortunate than I."

"I know you have," Lorna said quietly.

"And then Kit entered my life and felt like I had met my equal. There are few men that I like, Aunt Lorna, and fewer still that I respect. I admire Kit, and I respect him. His heart is for others, for me, I know it. Kit cares for me in a way that no other man has before. He makes me feel valued, as though I have a place at his side. I like spending time with him. I like listening to him. I know I could be a good version of myself with him. He makes me feel heard." Olivia took a deep breath. "You cannot know what it is to feel heard after all these years. He hears me, and he takes my voice and shouts it to those who will listen only to him.

"And I liked it. I do like it." Olivia paused. "I thought I liked it." Olivia looked down, feeling ashamed. "I wish it were me doing the shouting. I wish it were me that people were listening to. I wish it were me that could achieve the level of success that Kit is about to receive. I do not want to be merely at his side. I am so jealous of him and I hate myself for it." Olivia turned to her aunt. "Don't you see? I am wicked!"

Lorna frowned sadly. "Olivia, you are far from wicked," she promised. "I know how many people have told you no over the years. I have had enough conversations with county magistrates to understand the figures. What I take from what you just said is that you have found an equal in Kit. Isn't that wonderful?"

"Of course it is wonderful," Olivia said tearfully. "But it is also horrible. I am watching him succeed in the life that I wanted for myself and it makes me jealous!"

"Olivia!" Lorna said firmly. "What you need to understand is that there are certain barriers that you cannot cross. It is life, unfortunately, and you may not like it but you have to get used to it! You will never be permitted into a university or parliament, but you have the ability to inform. You have a voice, and Kit has listened to you! That is wonderful!" Lorna cried. "You have a place at his side, that is what it will look like to those who do not know you, but if Kit respects you and listens to you as you say, he will lift you up to his height and give you the ability to spread your good heart as far as it can go." Lorna placed her hand on Olivia's cheek. "I understand your turmoil, but it will pass, I promise. I know you, Olivia, and I know you will never change to suit any man. You need to find yourself a partner who loves every revolutionary part of you, who can celebrate your voice and not silence it."

It will pass? Would it? Olivia hoped so. This feeling was festering inside her like a disease.

Olivia knew that Kit would love every part of her if she let him. She knew that she could love every part of him if she allowed herself to. There was a potential for happiness in that future if she chose it.

"Don't run, Olivia," Lorna admonished. "Make the right decision. I know you know what that is."

The right decision. Olivia nodded. Kit was the right decision for her. She knew it. These feelings would go away, like Aunt Lorna said.

Lorna kissed Olivia's forehead. "Come now. Papa will be rising soon. We are to exchange gifts."

Lorna left her and Olivia returned her eyes to her reflection. "Choose happiness, Olivia," she willed herself.

She was joined shortly after by a maid who helped her to dress and fixed her hair for the day. Once ready, Olivia journeyed down to her grandfather's den in order to take part in the gift exchange.

The room was toasty warm thanks to the crackling fire. Her grandfather was sitting in his chair like always, tea beside him, and a book in his hand. Lorna was sorting out cups for Olivia and herself.

When Bernard noticed that Olivia had joined them he put down his book and offered her a cheerful smile. "My dear, happy Christmas!"

Olivia kissed her grandfather's forehead. "Happy Christmas, Grandpapa," she replied warmly.

There was a small pile of parcels on the table in front of the settee. Once everyone was seated, Lorna began to hand them out.

She read the first label. "To Papa, from Colin and family." Lorna handed the parcel to Bernard who read the label himself.

"Oh, it's from Colin!" Bernard cried happily having not heard Lorna. "Such a shame they couldn't travel. Blasted weather. Such luck you were able to join us Olivia." Bernard unwrapped the gift from his son and made a satisfied noise when it was revealed to be an ivory pipe.

"What a gift for an old man, Colin," Lorna chastised her brother under her breath.

Olivia lifted up the next parcel and read the label:

To the loveliest woman I have ever laid eyes on. Season's Greetings. F. Kelly.

Olivia frowned. "F. Kelly?"

Lorna jumped and immediately snatched the parcel from Olivia's hands.

Olivia suddenly remembered the name of the last magistrate who had arrested her. The handsome Mr Kelly who had paid some scandalous attention to her aunt. Olivia was sure she had teased Lorna about it at the time. Was something going on?

"What is it?" asked Olivia curiously. "Is he your ...?"

"Hush now, Olivia, not in front of Papa. It would break his heart." Lorna stuffed the gift behind her and quickly moved on to the next present in the pile.

It was then that Olivia realised just how much her aunt cared for her grandfather and how much her grandfather relied upon Lorna. Was Lorna not allowed to be happy while Bernard was alive?

Olivia was lucky. Selfishly so. She could do whatever she please ... within reason.

"This is from me, for you, Olivia." Lorna smiled as she handed the next parcel to Olivia.

"No, I will not be kept in a drawing room in my own house!" cried a voice from in the hall.

The hair suddenly stood up on the back of Olivia's neck. She knew that critical, loathsome tone anywhere.

"Mama," she whispered.

Chapter 19

Olivia immediately felt like a frightened little girl when her mother entered the den. She had not seen her mother in four years, and yet nothing had changed. Every insecurity, every faux pas she was suddenly so aware of. The hurt of knowing she would never have the love and approval of her mother was suddenly so prominent in her heart, as it had been the day she had been rejected at fifteen.

Ruth was as beautiful and as regal as ever. She was dressed immaculately, as a Countess should, in the finest travelling clothes money could buy. Her red hair was still perfect in colour, and her ivory skin did not betray her age. Her eyes, though, were filled with ire and judgement, and they were settled on her nineteen year old daughter.

"Away with you," Ruth said dismissively to the butler, Stoughton, who had obviously been trying to keep their guest to a drawing room so he could warn the family.

Bernard, whose chair was not facing the door, was still unaware that his eldest daughter had joined them. He was still happily inspecting the pipe he had received from Colin.

Lorna immediately put a comforting arm around Olivia but it did little to steady her nerves. Ruth noticed the action and looked upon them disapprovingly.

"Happy Christmas, sister," Lorna greeted tensely.

Ruth ignored her younger sister's well-wish. "I thought you might have returned here for Christmas and I was right." She immediately entered the room properly so that she was standing beside her father's chair, standing directly opposite Olivia and Lorna.

Now that Ruth was standing beside him, Bernard noticed her presence. He appeared quite shocked, and stared up at his eldest child. Ruth did not acknowledge him, just as she ignored Lorna.

"Wasn't it enough that your father and I had to explain to our friends that our daughter was off getting herself arrested instead of behaving like the proper lady she was brought up to be? Wasn't it enough that you were humiliating us in front of our friends? No? You felt it necessary to humiliate us in front of the entire country!" Ruth shouted furiously.

Olivia recoiled just as far back as the sofa would allow. It had been four years since her mother had last berated her and it felt just as terribly now as it did then.

Ruth took a deep breath and pinched the bridge of her nose. "I could have found you a suitable husband, someone with a position and respect. But no, marriage is too traditional for the likes of radical Olivia Pendleton. She feels it is more appropriate to be a politician's whore than a gentleman's wife!" Ruth sucked in an icy breath. "Tell me why, Olivia. Why do you hate me so? I raised you exactly the same way that Lady Gregson raised her daughter, who I was told at tea the other day is with child! Married to a Captain in the Navy and expecting! I all but had to show Lady Gregson the front page of the newspaper to tell her what my daughter was up to." Ruth clenched her fists and shook her head, her eyes narrowing on Olivia. "And with a Kensington of all people."

Olivia closed her eyes for a moment as her mother took a breath from her lecture. This was not the first time it was assumed that she was Kit's whore and not his advisor. What a nasty mistake it was to make, and it hurt even more coming from her mother. Her mother's words felt like bullets, insult after insult, bullet after bullet, hitting her right in the chest.

Olivia thought back to the dinner she had Kit had attended at the Hadley's. The same assumption had been made but the gentlemen at the table and Kit had defended her.

"I would wager you would not find fifty minds in the House of Commons who are as bright or enlightened as she is."

No matter her struggle with jealously, she was at Kit's side for a reason.

"Now Ruth –" Lorna began in Olivia's defence but Olivia interrupted her.

Olivia rose up from the settee and faced her mother. "I am Kit's political advisor, Mama," she said firmly. "I care not for what those newspapers have to say about me, but my role is clear. I am bright. I am enlightened. Kit chooses to take my advice because, as he says, you would not find fifty minds in the House of Commons who are as clever as me. That is something to be proud of, I think." Olivia puffed out her chest a little. It was something to be proud of.

Ruth continued to stare at her.

"I do not hate you, Mama. If only you knew how that were true. I am just different from you. I have ambitions and dreams that go beyond being married to a bloody naval captain!"

"Language!" spat Ruth. She turned her attention to Lorna. "This is your fault. You coddle her. Just like you were coddled."

Lorna gasped. "I do not coddle her!" she retorted, standing up from the settee. "I have very little influence over Olivia, I think. But at least I am here to try to influence her."

"Of course you are. Precious Lorna," Ruth mocked. "You wouldn't know discipline if it slapped you in the face. That is why I am the witch and you are the beloved aunt."

"Mama!" cried Olivia. "Do not be angry with Aunt Lorna when it is me you came to see."

"Quiet, Olivia," snapped Ruth.

"Do you have something to say to me, sister?" Lorna asked expectantly, clearly becoming angry and upset at Ruth's accusations.

Ruth smiled almost wickedly. "Oh, I have many things I would like to say to you, sister. To him, too," she said, nodding down towards her father. Bernard had returned to inspecting his pipe, taking no notice of the conflict.

"Then please, pray tell!" Lorna said exasperatedly.

"Perfect, precious Lorna can do no wrong."

"What are you talking about?" Lorna demanded to know.

"Didn't you ever question why Father doted on you so, and couldn't care a wit about me? But I am sure you mail his many letters to me, don't you? I am sure you were the one who sent off his Christmas gift for John and I, weren't you?"

Lorna was silent.

"No, I didn't think so," Ruth said condescendingly.

"He doesn't talk about you," replied Lorna quietly. "We don't talk about you. I don't know why."

"You never thought to question it? Or were to you too busy enjoying being the favourite child?"

"There is no need to be nasty, Ruth!" exclaimed Lorna. "That is why Papa doesn't include you. You are nasty! I am sure Olivia, and Papa, would welcome you with open arms if only you would be a little nicer!"

Olivia knew this conversation was not going to end well. Ruth was baiting her sister and Lorna was taking it. Ruth was not in the mood for reconciliation. She was here to fight.

"Come with me, Mama," Olivia announced as she marched over from the settee and took her mother's hand. Olivia dragged Ruth from the den and into the hallway, leading her down the corridor towards her own bedroom. Ruth followed her.

Once inside her bedroom, Olivia's released her mother's hand and closed the door.

Ruth was still so angry. "My father," she fumed, pointing in the direction of the den, "hated my mother. When she died I think he was glad. He was happy working, entertaining, letting nannies raise me instead of him. I wasn't always this bitter, Olivia, I hope you realise that," she snapped. "He told me once I reminded him of my mother. I understood exactly what he meant. You can imagine my ire when he married their mother and doted upon Colin and Lorna. Especially his precious angel, Lorna."

"I understand, Mama," Olivia replied softly. She had heard the story in bits and pieces over the years. Ruth hardly mentioned her family, but when she did it was with bitterness and envy.

They both sat down on Olivia's bed and faced each other. Olivia could see the hurt in her mother's eyes and it frightened her more than anything. She was so used to seeing her mother angry. She was not prepared for pain.

"I swore that when I became a mother I would never make my child feel as I did when I was a girl. I was going to raise her, to be there for her like my father should have been there for me. Nannies were not going to take my role. I made sure you have the best of everything. I ensured you had beautiful clothes, beautiful possessions. You had fine tutors. You learned languages and dancing and music. But nothing I did was right. You fought me at every turn. You hated me when all I ever did was try to give you the life I didn't have. You punished me, Olivia. You continue to punish me."

Olivia could feel the weight of the betrayal her mother felt sitting directly on her shoulders. She understood why her mother felt that way, but she had never known her mother cared so much about her. She had never felt that from Ruth, ever.

"Do you still care about me, Mama?" Olivia asked. She could not fathom the fear she felt behind this question. How could she handle another rejection?

Ruth softened a fraction. "I am your mother," she replied. "I am cursed to fret about you for the rest of my days."

Olivia could have beamed. She knew that was her mother's icy way of saying that she loved her. "I love you, Mama. I never meant to punish you. I never thought about how my actions would affect you or hurt you. I am simply doing what I feel is right. I am being a champion for those who have no-one. I have a clever head on my shoulders. You did not raise a fool."

"You were always too smart for your own good," Ruth said stiffly.

Olivia knew that her mother would never approve of her behaviour unless it involved vows and a church. But she hoped that they now understood each other in a way they had never been able to before.

"You really ought to get married," her mother continued. "Preferably to someone who could shut you up once in a while."

"I could never be married to someone who would want to quieten me," declared Olivia.

"I thought as much," murmured Ruth. "What am I going to tell your father then? He reads the newspaper and he is just as concerned about your reputation as I am."

"Tell him there is to be an election on the tenth of January, and his daughter is the advisor to a future MP," Olivia said proudly. "It is the truth, no matter what the newspapers decide to write."

Ruth shook her head. "She couldn't just be a debutante," she muttered under her breath.

And that was about as much acceptance as Olivia knew she was going to get from Ruth. Olivia smiled at her mother. Ruth rolled her eyes.

There was to be an election on the tenth of January, and Olivia knew of one other family who needed to know about it.

Chapter 20

R uth did not stay. There were too many hard feelings between her and her family for them all to be resolved in a day. For her daughter at least, things seemed better. She parted with Olivia on terms that were not as hostile as they had been four years ago. They seemed to have a new understanding for each other.

"Write to me, Olivia, so I have your address wherever you settle," Ruth murmured. She liked to keep her tone cool but Olivia sensed the genuine maternal concern in her mother's voice. "You know where Papa and I live, and you are welcome to visit." That almost sounded kind. Ruth quickly added, "Just write to us before. It is polite, you know."

Olivia hugged her mother tightly. She remembered practically scolding Kit when he was harsh towards her mother. Ruth was not a warm or particularly kind woman, but she was the only mother Olivia had, and she loved her anyway. All these years she had thought Ruth didn't care about her. This visit had proven otherwise, and Olivia felt such relief.

Ruth carefully patted Olivia's back in return. "Come now. I have a journey ahead of me."

"Are you sure you will not stay, Mama? Not even for dinner?"

Ruth shook her head. "No. Much needs to be said before I sit down to dinner with my father and siblings," she said coldly.

Olivia held her tongue, but she wished her mother would not hold such a grudge towards her kind aunt. Lorna was nearly two decades younger than Ruth after all, she had been too young to carry much of the blame for what happened.

Ruth left, and shortly after, Olivia departed as well, letting her aunt know that she would return before sundown. Lorna had protested but it was something that Olivia needed to do.

She asked the carriage to take her to Norwood Cottage, the estate belonging to Kit's family. She knew it would be quite an imposition to visit on Christmas, and they might be sensitive to her presence anyway, but she could not stay away. Having now reconciled, in a way, with her mother, Olivia wanted to speak with Kit's father.

The carriage pulled into the gates of Norwood Cottage around lunchtime. Cottage really was a silly name for such a grand, manor house. What it must have been for Kit growing up here. It looked even more magical with the soft snow that had settled on the green overnight.

The carriage stopped in front of the entry steps and the driver helped Olivia from the carriage. The front door had not yet opened, so Olivia journeyed up the steps and knocked on the large, oak door. She could hear the noise echoing inside.

Olivia suddenly felt a flurry of nerves settle in her stomach. She had come with good intentions but she knew that Kit's family did not like her. His father, at least, held a great prejudice against her because of her parents. Olivia hoped that her aunt still had affection for her.

Olivia had been standing at the front door for nearly two minutes before it was opened. She immediately was standing before Cassian.

Olivia found him to be intimidating. He was tall, not as tall as Kit was, but much taller than her, and his eyes were charcoal black and hard, especially when they settled upon a Pendleton. His mouth was rigid and his jaw was tense and his brows immediately furrowed.

Olivia never minded what people thought of her. But she minded that Cassian did not like her. She minded a lot, and she wanted to change his mind.

Upon looking at him more closely, as Cassian continued to look down at her, she could see more emotion in his face. His black eyes were hard, but they were sad, and she could see the shadows under his eyes. They were very pronounced, indicating that he had not had a very good night's sleep in a long while.

Olivia cleared her throat nervously. "Good afternoon, Mr Kensington," she greeted timidly.

"Good afternoon, Miss Olivia," he replied coolly. Olivia could not help but notice Cassian subtly looking over her head towards the carriage that she had arrived in. He had to be looking for Kit. When he realised that she had come alone she could only see the sadness in him increase. "What are you doing here?" A sudden wave of panic came across Cassian's face. "Is my son alright?" he demanded to know.

"Yes!" cried Olivia reassuringly. "We parted nearly a week ago for Christmas. He is spending the holiday with Prince Edward in

London," she explained. "I returned to spend Christmas with my grandfather and aunt."

"Oh," was all he said in reply. Olivia's heart bled for him. He was so disappointed. Cassian opened the door wider for her to enter. "You may take the horses around to the stable," he called out to the driver. "You will find water and hay there."

Olivia crossed the threshold and entered into the foyer. She could hear Kit's family nearby. They sounded merry, or at least the children did.

Faith took a deep breath and faced Cassian. "I wanted to speak with you and Aunt An – Faith, if I could, please," she asked, her voice quivering.

Cassian nodded. "I am sure your aunt would like to see you," he replied quietly. "Follow me." Cassian led Olivia down a hallway towards, what Olivia presumed was, a dining room. When he opened the door, she was greeted by a sitting room.

Inside, Faith and Kit's two younger sisters were sitting on the floor, on what looked like a bed sheet, with all sorts of dishes around them. It looked like a gourmet, indoor picnic.

All three pairs of eyes were immediately on Olivia. Faith's eyes immediately widened in amazement. "Olivia!" she cried. "Cassian," Faith lifted up her arms, "come and help me to stand."

Olivia frowned, but only for a moment. Cassian helped his wife up to her feet, and Olivia could immediately see the reason why. She was very pregnant. Olivia wondered how long she had to go before she had her baby.

Faith waddled around the furniture to where Olivia was standing by the door. Olivia had always thought her aunt very pretty, beautiful even, but she, like Cassian, looked tired, and there was sadness in her brown eyes, too.

Kit did not know how much his family were missing him.

Faith pulled Olivia into her arms for a hug. The minute her aunt's round belly touched Olivia's she jumped backwards as though she had been kicked. Faith rubbed her stomach and uttered, "Don't be rude," to her child. "How are you, dear?"

Olivia could hear the second question in her aunt's voice. She was asking after Kit as well. "I am well," she replied, "and so is he."

Faith smiled, and immediately turned away. Olivia caught a glimpse of her eyes as they became glassy. Faith cleared her throat. "Olivia, I do not believe you have been properly introduced to our daughters," she announced, changing the subject. "Girls, stand up," she encouraged.

Olivia remembered Lucy. She had met once before when she and Kit had once met. She recalled the smaller daughter from when she and Kit had left Norwood nearly four months ago but she did not know her name.

"This is Lucy," said Faith, placing her hand on Lucy shoulders. Lucy was a very pretty girl who looked very much like her mother. Brown eyes, shiny brown hair, and the same calm disposition.

Olivia felt that she knew too much about Lucy, really. She had heard it all from her parents growing up. She was really the child of Olivia's late Uncle George, but Faith was choosing to raise her illegitimate to keep the Pendletons from having anything to do with Lucy. For Faith to bring such disadvantage upon her own child her uncle must have been an even more vicious creature than she could remember.

"I'll be eleven in six weeks," Lucy informed her. "On St. Valentine's Day."

Olivia smiled. Was she hinting for a gift? "A very good day for a birthday."

"And this is Emma," Faith introduced their younger daughter. Emma was very obviously the child of Cassian. Same black eyes. Same curly, black hair. Olivia was convinced in Emma was five feet taller and looking down at Olivia, her stare would be just as intimidating as her father's. "Girls, this is my niece, Olivia."

"What is she to us?" asked Lucy.

Olivia was certain Cassian would have conniptions if his own children were cousins to a Pendleton, so she replied with, "A friend."

A bark suddenly alerted Olivia to a dog that was lounging on one of the settees in the sitting room. It was a King Charles spaniel, and a very pretty dog, indeed.

"And that's Cat," added Faith. "The result of a toddler being in charge of the name." She laughed to herself. Olivia could not help but smirk.

"Olivia would like to talk to us," murmured Cassian to Faith.

Faith nodded knowingly. "Girls, keep eating, and do not feed your dinners to Cat," she warned. "Let us go out in the hall."

Once the door was closed and they were alone in the hallway, Olivia began. "I know that Kit's actions have hurt you both terribly," she said apologetically. "I have only recently, today actually, come to understand pain from a parent's perspective." How could Olivia form the words without Cassian hating her more than he already did? "It was my doing," she admitted. She was wrong. He could hate her more. "When I was in gaol," Faith's eyes widened, "and I was watching his behaviour around you I called him on it. I asked why he was so blindly following you, walking on eggshells around you. I did not have much in the way of respect for one's elders at the time so it was nothing to me to go against one's parents. But it started Kit thinking and that is why he made the decision he did.

"I don't know if you know this, but Kit and I met once before when we were children. I was eleven at the time, and you both were visiting my parents for some reason or another. But I asked Kit to help me steal some books from my father to fill the little library I was creating for the village school. Kit told me how you taught him to read, and how he was an example of what good could come out of giving the poor a chance."

"I didn't know that," replied Cassian quietly. "Kit never mentioned that he met you."

"Probably because you declared all Pendletons messengers from the devil or something like that," quipped Faith. Cassian threw Faith an exasperated look.

"Mr Kensington, I don't know what happened in the past. Aunt, I can only imagine, and I don't like to," Olivia said sincerely, "but please do not judge me for the sins of my parents. I love my parents, but I do not like or agree with everything that they do or have done. I cannot choose who my parents are. But Kit did. He is so lucky, and he knows that he is."

"Olivia, I know my behaviour must seem unfair, and it is, I know it, but you cannot understand. You were a child. Watching my wife endure ..." Cassian trailed off as though it was too painful for him to continue.

"What Cassian means is that we do not know the same people that you do, Olivia," explained Faith. "And Cassian fears that having you in our lives means having your parents involved as well."

The little hope that Olivia had built up for winning Cassian Kensington over was suddenly dashed. She would always be one of them in his eyes.

"I did not come here for selfish reasons," said Olivia, brushing away the hurt. "I just wanted to tell you that your son has been making you proud these last months. Kit is kind and decent and unlike any other gentleman I have ever encountered. He is fighting for people, for causes that he believes in. Education, for instance, which is something that you placed in his heart as a boy, Mr Kensington. Not only that, but he is ever so clever. So smart, he holds his own against truly vile men who would only see him fail. He negotiates and ensures the result is fair. I trust he gets his business sense from you, sir." Perhaps Olivia was still trying to win him over a little. Olivia turned her attention to Faith. Softly, she said, "He defended you, Aunt, when people would soil your name, just like you know he would. When a man dishonoured you he fought for your good name and your excellent character, he defended his beloved mother."

Faith did not hide the tears in her eyes this time. She removed a handkerchief from the sleeve of her dress and immediately dried her eyes. Cassian put a comforting arm around her.

"And what of your name?" asked Cassian. "What does he say to that?"

"What do you mean?" asked Olivia.

"The newspapers reach us here, as well," replied Cassian. "Just because he is away from home does not mean I am not aware of his whereabouts and behaviour."

Olivia realised he was referencing how the newspapers were representing her. "Well, that same man managed to dishonour me in the same sentence and Kit was just as gallant in my defence as he was my aunt's."

Olivia could see that Cassian was fearful that there was truth in the words the reporters wrote. He was worried that his son was behaving dishonourably. He should know better.

"Kit has only ever behaved like a perfect gentleman towards me, something that I am wholly unused to. I am used to being laughed at when I try to speak, to being jeered and insulted and dismissed. Kit is the first man to actually listen to what I have to say. You ought to be proud of him, Mr Kensington."

"I always was," he murmured.

There was still so much hurt in this house. Olivia knew she could not fix it on her own. She had not come to fix it, only to help. "I know that he wants to see you both, see you all," she promised, "only he knows not what to say. I am sure when he has the words he will explain everything. You are too precious to him not to resolve things."

"You are a good friend to him, Olivia," said Faith, "and a good person so speak to us like this when I know it must be difficult to face disapproval."

"I try to be. I try to do all things good but my abilities can only extend so far. If you only knew the achievement that Kit was about to make. He is about to be elected to parliament! He will have a say, a voice within the most powerful house in the country, to make things better for people like Kit when he was a child." Olivia looked up at Cassian pleadingly. "The election is to be held on the tenth of January. I know all is not well and everything is not alright yet, but I know it would mean the world to Kit if you were there, sir."

Cassian did not give her an answer. He merely looked down at her silently for a moment. "Thank you for bringing us this information, Olivia," he said after a minute. "You really ought to get back to your family. With the election so soon, you will not have much longer with them."

Olivia smiled hopefully. "You will come?"

"Good afternoon, Olivia," Cassian said dismissively as he led Faith back towards the sitting room. "We will ring the bell for your carriage."

Even though the sitting room door was now closed, Olivia could still hear their muffled voices from inside.

"I suppose I will have to get used to having a Pendleton in the house," said Cassian.

"Perhaps you will not mind so much when her name is Kensington," replied Faith playfully.

Olivia froze. That was what they had taken from her plea? All she had done was ... explain in great detail how wonderful Kit was to his parents. The two people on earth who knew exactly how wonderful he was.

What was she going to do? How was she going to feel when she faced Kit again? Would the jealousy simply go away, as Lorna had said, and she could be happy with Kit? Or would this only make them both miserable?

Chapter 21

Kit leapt out of his chair in the dining room of the inn when he saw through the window Olivia emerging from her carriage. It had been far too long since he had last seen her.

If he had learned anything during their parting from one another, it was that he preferred to be in her company than without it. Christmas at the Palace was extraordinary, but he would take an intimate conversation with Olivia any day.

Kit practically pulled the door off its hinges in order to meet her outside.

Olivia was fixing her travelling cloak. She wore her hair down for travelling, and the brisk January wind was blowing it across her face. Just that image of her, with her hair windswept as it was, made her look as beautiful as he had ever seen her.

Kit could not wait for this election to be over. He wanted to win, of course, but he wanted to properly court Olivia. He did not want any more of the abhorrent speculation about her. Kit wanted to court her, and when the time was right, he wanted to propose and marry her.

Kit knew that Olivia would love Westminster. She would love the power and influence that she would have as an MP's wife. She would be able to achieve more than she could have ever dreamed.

And they could be happy together. Kit knew that Olivia would make him happy. He only hoped that he could make her happy as well.

"Olivia!" he cried.

Olivia looked up at him and she smiled brightly. Kit would never tire of her smile. "Kit!" Olivia closed the distance between them quickly and hugged him tightly.

Kit found himself holding her close, his arms fixed around her waist and, bending over due to his height, his head resting on top of hers. He could smell the scented soap in her hair still.

Olivia moved her head and looked up at him. In their present position they were only inches from each other. Olivia's eyes softened as she looked at him. Her brows furrowed slightly and she looked slightly conflicted.

"What is it?" he asked her quietly.

"I saw your parents while I was in Derbyshire," she told him, though something in his gut was telling him that this was not the only thing that was on her mind.

Kit pulled away only slightly, still keeping an arm around her waist as he led her inside and out of the cold. "You did?" was all he could manage to say in reply. He and Olivia sat down at the table he had been occupying before.

"They are both well," she assured him.

Kit knew that. His mother's letter at Christmas had assured him that they were all in good health. How could he ask Olivia if his father was still furious with him without looking like a coward?

"They miss you," she continued softly.

"Did he say that?"

Olivia pursed her lips. That had to mean no. "Well, not exactly," she admitted, "but you ought to have seen his face when he saw I was alone. He was so sad. He wanted to see you."

Kit could imagine his father wouldn't have admitted anything to Olivia. He was too preoccupied with his prejudices against her to see the good deed she was trying to do in calling upon them. "You have such a good heart, Olivia," he complimented sincerely. "I appreciate you visiting them. It must not have been easy knowing how my father feels about your family."

Olivia brushed it off. "I understand his feelings," replied Olivia.

Kit did as well to a certain degree. But Olivia did not deserve to be shut out because of her relations.

A frightening though suddenly occurred to him. Kit wanted to reconcile with his parents, it was only a matter of time, but what would happen if he and Olivia became engaged? Would his father truly never accept her? Would they indeed have to become strangers?

Olivia interrupted his thoughts. "But I did see my mother while I was in Derbyshire, also." This news seemed to make Olivia happier.

Olivia's mother was often a taboo subject growing up in his father's house. But in conversing with Olivia, it was clear that she still loved her mother no matter her sins, and Ruth's rejection had impacted on her a great deal.

"Did it go well?"

Olivia nodded happily. "Oh, yes. Mama and I spoke civilly, and I think we understood some of our differences. She cares about me, Kit." Olivia smiled. "My mother cares."

Such a simple action, which ought to be thoughtless, effortless for any parent, but to Olivia it meant so much. If she was happy, then so was he.

"I am really proud of you, Olivia," Kit said sincerely. "Not only for speaking with my parents, but for overcoming your differences with your mother. You truly are remarkable."

Kit enjoyed Olivia's cheeks becoming rosy.

"In fact, you are indispensable to me. This absence has proven that to me. I don't ever want to be parted from you again." Where this nerve was coming from, Kit didn't know, but he was glad he was able to finally voice his feelings, a subject they had been dancing around for months.

Olivia's posture straightened in her chair. Her cheeks were fully flushed and she seemed to be a quite nervous in hearing his words. She looked how he felt.

Just a little more courage, Kit, he was telling himself as he continued. "When the election is over, regardless of the result, I want to treat you properly. I want to court you, and do all the things a young couple ought to do before they wed, whilst conquering Westminster together should the result be in our favour."

Olivia honestly looked petrified. But perhaps this was how all girls behaved when they were approached romantically by a man. She visibly took a deep breath and said, "I asked my aunt about this. I have very little experience in such matters. She told me to make the right decision, and I would know what it was." Olivia looked at him very determined. "I believe you are my equal, Kit." She stood up from her chair, and just as she had done when Kit was fourteen, Olivia leaned over and pressed her lips to his.

And just as he had been when he was fourteen, Kit was embarrassingly unprepared. Just as Kit composed himself enough to cup her cheek and return her affections, Olivia pulled away.

"Now, we have an election to win, don't we?" She arched her brow.

The week leading up to the election was utter madness. Kit and Olivia spent their time canvassing and conversing with as many people as possible. They attended dinners and teas with voters and did their very best to ensure that the people of Hertford made the right choice.

They worked together beautifully, Olivia knew it. They were a wonderful team, and together they could make wonderful things happen. The jealousy was still there, nestled in the pit of her stomach. She had not told Kit about it, not wanting him to think ill of her. But Olivia was just hoping that it would go away just like Aunt Lorna said it would.

Lorna had advised Olivia to make the right choice. Kit was the right choice. If there was ever a man a girl like her ought to marry, it would be him.

The tenth of January arrived quickly. It was a day of great excitement in Hertford. The vote was being held in the courthouse.

Olivia was dressed in the finest gown she had brought with her, the red dress she was particularly fond of. Kit, too, was dressed in his very best suit. Olivia helped him to tie his cravat as he was too nervous to stop his hands from shaking.

"But to hear them vote openly against me..." Kit trailed off.

Votes could not be concealed. The gentlemen would reveal to the room just who they were casting their vote for.

"You have done everything you can," assured Olivia. "They would be fools not to elect you."

"Even if I lose, you will still think well of me?"

Olivia could not believe he actually feared that. "You could do several things worse than losing an election and I would still consider you the best man I know," she promised. "Now, come. These votes are not going to cast themselves."

Olivia and Kit left the inn and much the same time as everyone else in town was leaving their homes and abandoning their businesses for the vote. Kit was stopped and talked to several time, and it took them a good half hour to make their way to the courthouse.

Those not eligible to vote, being of poor means or being female, waited outside in the huge developing crowd. The sheer number of bodies made it seem warm on this cold January day.

Kit and Olivia pushed their way to the front so that they could enter the court. The door was being manned by a tall, burly fellow.

He looked kindly on Kit. "Sir Christopher," he greeted politely. But his gaze was much more unfavourable when it fell on Olivia. "No women," he barked.

"Miss Pendleton is my advisor," Kit argued. "She must be permitted."

"I'm sorry, sir," he said firmly. "The law is clear. No women."

Olivia refused to let herself be smothered by all that she had been trying to repress. She wouldn't become upset. She would not be jealous of Kit's day. Women were not allowed in the vote, it was alright, it was the law. She did not have to make a scene or ruin Kit's day.

Olivia put on a fake smile. "You go on, I insist," she urged. "I will be out here cheering for you."

Kit looked so reluctant to part from her, but nevertheless he entered the vote and the door was closed in her face.

Olivia swallowed her pride and returned to the crowd. There were all sorts of people standing around her. High born ladies, low born men, woman and children. They were all people that she wanted to help. She and Kit could help them. She did not have to be in that room to help them, did she?

"Vote Kit!"

Olivia jumped when a cheeky voice whispered that in her ear. She turned around to see Prince Edward hiding himself under a cloak and hood. He was grinning mischievously.

"Your Royal Highness," greeted Olivia.

Just as she went to curtsey to him, Edward stopped her. "None of that. I am incognito. My father would have a fit if it was known I was at an election. We are above politics, you see."

Olivia smiled. "Well, I am glad you broke your father's rule to be here. Kit will be grateful to have your support, even if it is in secret."

"How long does it take to hear a result anyhow?" asked Edward.

"I don't know," admitted Olivia. "I've never really been at an election long enough to hear a result. I always find myself arrested within ten minutes."

Edward laughed. "You are an interesting character, aren't you? I can clearly see why Kit is in love with you."

Olivia looked away from the prince to hide her blushing cheeks. She knew that Kit was in love with her, even if he had not said the words yet.

Olivia and Edward conversed for the next half an hour while they waited outside the court for the result. The people didn't seem restless though. Ale was being poured around. Others were hawking their goods. Children were selling sweets.

But finally the door opened and the voters emerged. Kit and his opponent, Lawrence Powell, were the last to emerge. The gentlemen all stood before the crowd that had congregated to hear the result.

But Olivia could already tell who had won just by the look in Kit's eyes.

Mr Frank Hadley addressed the crowd, "With seventy percent of the vote, Hertford has a new MP!" he shouted to the people. "May I present the Honourable Sir Christopher Kensington!"

The crowd erupted into applause and cheers. Olivia and Edward joined them, clapping and cheering at Kit's triumph.

Kit stepped forth and shook Mr Hadley's hand. He then stood in front of the men and motioned for the crowd to settle. "Thank you!" he cried gratefully. "I am honoured to represent you in Westminster as your MP."

Before Kit could say anything further, Lawrence Powell stepped forward angrily. "His mother is a whore!" he roared to the crowd. "And his sister is a bastard! Is this who you want representing you in London?"

Powell was pulled away by the men as the crowd jeered him. Kit did not look overcome by the outburst, merely more determined.

"I am honoured to represent you in London," Kit continued. "My mother is a wonderful woman, and my sister is an innocent. The day a man is judged not by the circumstances of his birth, but by the quality of his character is the day England will be the greatest country in the world. You have made the right decision in putting your trust in me today. I will endeavour to do you all proud."

The crowd once again erupted in cheers and applause. Olivia beamed proudly as she turned her head to take in the crowd. Everyone seemed so proud of Kit. Some more than most. Her eyes found a lone man standing in the back of the crowd. He was clapping, and Olivia could see that he had tears in his eyes.

"He came," breathed Olivia. "Excuse me," she said to Edward as she pushed through the crowd to get to the back.

Cassian was at the very back of the crowd, hiding almost, wearing dark travelling clothes and a tricorn hat. But he had come, and he looked prouder than ever. Cassian smiled at Olivia when he noticed her emerging from the crowd. It was the warmest gesture she had ever received from him.

Behind her, Olivia could hear that Mr Hadley was singing Kit's praises.

"I did not think you would come," Olivia said to Cassian once she had reached him.

"This is an important moment in his life, Olivia," Cassian replied. "When you are a father, it is your responsibility to be present for these moments. Bur for me, it is my pleasure. There is anger between Kit and me, but I won't have him in years to come thinking that his father didn't care enough to be there on the big days in his life. I will always be here for him, not matter any ill feeling. I am proud. That boy, that man," he corrected, "up there is my son."

Olivia never saw a prouder father. There were tears in Cassian's black eyes and his cheeks looked like they ought to hurt from smiling. "You are a good father, Mr Kensington. Your children are lucky."

Cassian laughed lightly at the notion. "I try to be, Olivia. I am not always successful, and I make mistakes as you know. But I want my children to know that they have my support and that I care. I love them. Kit knows I love him."

"Come and speak to him." Olivia motioned for Cassian to follow her. "I am sure Kit will want to see you."

But Cassian shook his head. "Not today," he said. "Today is his day. I don't want to ruin it when there is still much to be said between us. When he is ready to come home I will tell him I was here." The proud smile did not leave his face. "That's my boy," he said to himself. "Go and celebrate with him, Olivia," Cassian urged. "Congratulations."

Olivia would keep the secret for now. She was so glad that Cassian had made the decision to come despite the fact that he and Kit needed to have a serious discussion before they could reconcile.

But now it was time to celebrate. Kit was going to Westminster. And Olivia would go with him.

Olivia stood in the crowd again and cheered and applauded. It did not matter to her that she would not be allowed inside there either, did it?

Olivia shook off the thought and kept clapping. She could see Kit's eyes searching for her in the crowd. "Be happy, Olivia," she told herself. "Don't be selfish."

Chapter 22

- -

"Clearly the Member for Highbury is spouting nonsense!"

"Mr Speaker!" cried the Member for Highbury in retaliation. "It is imperative that we as a people keep the grain prices high in order to secure maximum profit from trade! Perhaps the Member for Northcote needs one or two lessons in economics?" he teased across the floor.

The energy in the House of Commons was electric. Kit was in absolute awe, and had been for the past month he had been in London. He was sitting only a few rows back from the Prime Minister, who was now out of his seat enforcing his party's stance on the price of grain, much to the chagrin of the Whigs, and adding to the migraine of the Speaker.

Kit had found much of parliamentary life to be arguing in the House, shouting across the room your position until it was time to retire for the day. The Whigs and the Tories seemed to be opposed on every single subject, and so one had to be prepared to put up a fight to pass any law.

Kit was learning every day. He was learning that it was not as easy as he had once thought to bring about social change once in parliament. He was young; possibly the youngest MP in the House, and so he was not experienced enough to put forth any of his own ideas yet. His role was to support his superiors, to gain their respect and support, before he could introduce any one of his ideas.

It was not easy either. Kit had a conscience, and there were many things that he might have had a different opinion on, but it was not the time yet.

The price of grain, for example, was a subject that Kit had an opinion on, and it was not one that reflected his party's. His heart said lower the price, but his head understood why they didn't want to.

These were small battles. The war was yet to be fought and won. Once he was able to introduce education reforms into parliament, the people of this country would be able to afford higher prices for grain.

Kit had been taken under the wing of Richard Ashcroft, one of the PM's ministers. Kit knew that he was seen as exciting within the party elders, the future of politics. His background excited them, particularly as he was the son of a self-made man and not a peer who had bought his son's way into the House. Kit was representative of the working man, or so they said, and would refresh and improve the image of the party.

Kit was happy to learn, and to pave the way to him having his say within the House.

When the House retired for the day, Kit met with Mr Ashcroft. Mr Ashcroft was older than Kit's father, at least by ten years or so.

He was a seasoned politician, having held his seat for the past two decades.

"Just a few more days I wager," mused Mr Ashcroft, "and we'll have a vote on this issue and we can move on to the next. You ought to join us at the Club this evening, Kensington. I am certain that your youth will liven up our smoking party."

Kit laughed nervously. "I thank you for the invitation, Mr Ashcroft, but I fear I am already engaged this evening." How literal he hoped that would be.

"Ah, pity. Tomorrow then." And Mr Ashcroft departed.

Kit did not think that he would ever move past the grandeur that was the Palace of Westminster. To think it was where he was now employed. Kit exited out into Central London, onto the street overlooking the River Thames.

It was early evening, and everyone seemed to be in a rush to get to their evening engagements. Kit looked over to a bench that overlooked the river. As usual, Olivia was sitting on it, looking out over the river.

Kit smiled, though she had not seen him yet. He placed his hand in his pocket and felt the ring that he had placed there this morning. Oh how he prayed this night would go well.

Olivia watched as a dirty great crate floated down the Thames. The water really was grotty. She wished that people would take better care of it.

Olivia was sitting on her usual bench outside the Houses of Parliament. It had become routine for her and Kit. He would go to work in Westminster in the morning, and Olivia would meet him on this bench each evening, where they would then go on to enjoy a play or dine at a restaurant. All sorts of normal activities for people who were courting.

What Olivia did during the day was her own business, which Kit did not often inquire after. Olivia usually spent her days walking. She knew the surrounding areas and streets backwards and forwards, sideways and back again. She could close her eyes and point out important structures with accuracy. She could tell you which little patisserie made the nicest scones.

What she could not tell you, though, was what on earth she was doing here.

Olivia had been meeting Kit on this bench for a month now. They had been in London a month. In that time, she had watched Kit flourish. She loved how much he loved parliament. She was so proud to see him succeed and to know she had a part in it.

But what she could not stand was sitting here on this bench waiting, or spending her days wandering around London, and doing nothing with her time. Olivia had such ambition, such vision for what she was to do with her life. And she was staring it most of the time. She was staring at the Houses of Parliament, watching others, watching Kit, do what she desperately wanted to.

Aunt Lorna had said the jealousy would go away. Olivia had tried to make the right decision. She had tried being the dutiful, patient partner of Kit. She had tried to suppress this jealousy and carry on as if nothing was wrong.

But something was terribly wrong. Olivia was not one to sit around waiting while others did the work she wanted to. Something had to change. And she was going to tell Kit tonight.

Olivia honestly did not know how their conversation was going to go. She did not know how Kit was going to understand that she had been effectively lying to him for months by not telling him how she was feeling. Would he hate her? Would he resent her? Olivia wouldn't blame him.

Olivia's role in Kit's parliamentary career was over. He did not need her anymore, and there was nothing wrong with that. But that did not mean that Olivia was content to live the life she had been living for the past month.

"Good evening."

Olivia had been so consumed in her own thoughts that she had not heard Kit approaching. She turned around quickly to see him standing before her, smiling down at her quizzically.

"Oh, you startled me," she gushed.

"Where was your head?" he asked curiously, his brow furrowing.

"It's a long story," she murmured. That was an understatement. "How was today?" she asked, patting the seat beside her.

Kit joined her on the bench. "Much the same as yesterday, and such will be tomorrow I expect. Arguing about the price of grain."

"It ought to be lowered," replied Olivia firmly. "Poor farmers cannot afford to purchase the grain they produce for their masters."

"I agree," nodded Kit. "But it's the position of the party that higher prices promote growth within trade. I cannot argue while I am still so inexperienced. When I introduce our education reform, everyone will be able to purchase grain."

Olivia appreciated that Kit said "our". Kit wanted to include her. But once again, Aunt Lorna had been right. There were certain barriers that she was not allowed to cross, and she had to get used to it.

There was nothing for her here. What a conclusion to realise. What a horrid thing to know. And wicked did that make her when Kit and his good heart were right here?

Olivia needed to tell him. She needed him to listen to her, as he always had, and she prayed he had a solution that could stop this gut-wrenching jealousy that was simply eating her up inside.

"Kit, I need to talk to you. I need to tell you something." Olivia's tone was suddenly so serious, and Kit took notice immediately.

Kit turned his body towards her properly and took her hand in his. He looked at her intently, the concern shining through his green eyes. "What is it?" he asked quietly, his voice thick with unease.

Olivia could feel the heavy emotion filling her throat. She was going to cry, she just knew it. She had to tell him the truth.

Olivia sucked in a breath. Here she went. About to ruin everything. "Kit," she whispered. "I'm not happy."

Kit recoiled slightly. "What do you mean?" he asked fearfully.

Olivia pulled her hand from his and buried her face. "I am not happy," she repeated. Tears began to full her eyes, just as she feared. "I haven't been happy for a long while. In fact, I have been experiencing such wicked, horrid jealousy for months."

To let out those words was oddly freeing, but to know she had put such a burden on Kit hurt her even worse. She dared not look at him. She was a coward, yet she kept going.

"I know it makes me a terrible person. I should be happy for you, and I am, I promise! But I had such plans for my life, such ambitions and dreams, you know this. I thought by helping you become elected it would help me in achieving my goal. But really all I have gained is an overwhelming wave of jealousy I feel towards you. I wish it were me shouting in parliament. I wish it were me with the power to introduce educational reform. I wish it were me that people would simply listen to. But it cannot be, and I need to comprehend this, I know." Olivia took a moment to breathe. Her voice was becoming hysterical with emotion. The cuffs of her dress were soaked in tears.

Kit had not placed a comforting arm around her. He was not touching her. Olivia wanted to have the courage to look at him but she couldn't.

"I do not want to be this person. I do not want to spend my days wasting time, waiting for you to finish in parliament. I want to be the little girl who steals books from her father's library to stock the school. I want to be the girl who takes money from her own dowry to pay for a teacher. Lord, I want to be arrested again and again knowing that I was fighting for what I believed in. I don't recognise myself anymore." Olivia gasped at that realisation. "I am not myself anymore."

Be brave, she willed herself. Olivia wiped her eyes with her cuffs and turned to look at Kit. He looked just as she felt. She could see the hurt in his eyes, the confusion and pain. His body was so tense and rigid. His lips were pressed firmly shut as he stared at her. She could see the redness in his eyes, as if his emotion was about to overcome him.

"I am not myself anymore," she told him softly. "My aunt told me that the jealousy would pass, and that you were the right choice for me. And I believed her. I believe her in the latter. I believe you are the right man for me, the only man, really, who would ever put up with me. But ..." Olivia's voice cracked. She could not believe that these words were coming out of her mouth. "I do not believe I am the right choice for you."

She watched as those words washed over Kit, hitting him just like a fist would. He blinked, once, twice, a third time, as he took in her words.

"Don't I get a say in this?" Kit asked after a moment of silence. His voice was thick with emotion, just like hers. Olivia could see the tears welling up in his eyes.

"Of course you do," replied Olivia. She willed him to change her mind. But she already knew it was made up.

Olivia watched as Kit suddenly dug into his pocket. His hand quickly emerged with a small ring. She gasped when she realised what it was. The ring, which was embellished with little green stones along the band, was beautiful, and it made Olivia hate herself even more than she already did.

"Do you know what this is?" he asked. "You are the right choice for me," he said determinedly. "I am right for you and you are right for me. I wish ... I wish you would have said something sooner. I wish I would have realised sooner. We could have figured it out together. Olivia, I only want to make you happy."

Olivia sobbed loudly. "But I cannot make you happy. How can you be happy with a miserable wife? I want more for my life than this bench." She slapped the stone she was sitting on. "And I want more for you than for you to be married to someone who is jealous of you."

"What is it you want then?" Kit's voice was not filled with anger fuelled hurt.

"I don't know yet. I haven't achieved it yet. But I know I want to. I want to seek it out. I want to pursue causes that I am passionate about. I want to wind up in a few more gaol cells!" she cried. "I know you are the right man for me, Kit. But I am not ready for you to be. And that is probably the most selfish thing I have ever said."

Kit nodded his head as he comprehended what she said. Olivia watched as he put the ring away. That hit her right in the stomach. It was a sudden realisation of her reality. This was it.

They both sat on the bench staring at one another. It was as if both of them were trying to memorise the other, to capture this moment and make sense of it. They loved it other, that was clear, but it was not that simple. Olivia knew that if they married she would wind up as one of those political wives that she and Kit had dined with in Hertford. She could help and advise him all she wanted at home, but that was not enough for her.

Olivia needed more. She was only nineteen years old, and she had a lot of fight left in her young body. "I am so sorry," she said after what felt like an age of silence.

"Don't apologise for being you, Olivia. I always thought you were extraordinary. You always told me you were going to change the world. If I have to let you go in order for you to do that then I will. I love you enough to do that."

Olivia loved Kit's kindness, but she knew he truly struggled to say those words.

The future was now ambiguous. Olivia had either made the best decision or the biggest mistake of her life. She leaned over and kissed Kit's cheek softly. She heard him suck in a breath as she did so. They both knew it was goodbye.

Chapter 23

Kit felt as if nothing would ever be as good as it once was. Olivia was gone. She had left. She had given up her room in the hotel they were staying in and she had left. She had climbed in a carriage and disappeared.

It wasn't just words. Her fears were not mere jitters. She had been completely serious and she had left him.

The feeling of being left behind was utterly bleak. It physically hurt, as if someone was stabbing him in the chest repeatedly. Kit mourned the life he had planned for himself and Olivia. It was almost like that person had died. He had honestly thought that he would be engaged to be married at this moment. And yet he wasn't. Olivia had been feeling all sorts of doubts for months and she had not told him. And God forgive him, he was so angry at her for it.

How could one person love, mourn and be angry at another all at once?

Kit had never experienced heartbreak before. He had never been in love before Olivia. He had never even thought that it would not work out perfectly. He had thought that she felt the same way about him.

In the back of his mind, Kit understood that Olivia did love him, she just was not ready for what Kit was ready for. He knew that the right thing to do was to let her go. She deserved to be happy, and if he could not make her happy then alas, c'est la vie.

But at this moment it was difficult to focus on the positive.

Kit had spent the next few weeks in a haze. He attended parliament each day but it was difficult to pay attention which was an added weight on his shoulders. How could he properly represent the people who elected him when he could not even concentrate on what was being argued about?

"You don't look well, Kensington. You haven't done for a while now. Are you ill?" commented Mr Ashcroft halfway through March.

Olivia had been gone for just over three weeks. Kit had not heard from her. She had not written to say she had arrived safe, wherever she had gone. It was another blow to know that there would be no contact, no communication with the person who had been his closest friend and confidante these last months.

Kit felt truly pathetic. There was nothing physically wrong with him, and yet his symptoms felt entirely physical. "A little under the weather," he replied, under exaggerating entirely.

"Take a few weeks," he instructed. "Go to Bath. You will feel better. Return refreshed ready to fight until the summer recess." Mr Ashcroft slapped him on the shoulder and left Kit.

Kit left parliament and found himself looking to the bench as he always did. Every time he saw it was empty, or worse, occupied by a couple, it hit him again. There were memories everywhere.

Kit was alone in London. He was alone and yet he had a very important job to do, and at the moment he was failing in that dismally. There was so much Kit wanted to achieve, and while he was feeling like this he was useless.

Mr Ashcroft was right. Kit needed to leave for a little while. But not to Bath. He needed to go home. He did not have anyone in London, but he had people in Derbyshire.

Kit needed his family.

Five days later, Kit found himself travelling through the gates of Norwood Cottage. Had he really not been here since September?

Kit could not believe how much time had passed. He had not really noticed it much while he was spending time planning with Olivia.

But it had been half a year since he had seen his family. Half a year. How could he have let this ill feeling carry on for so long? How could he have treated his family in such a way?

And yet here he was, in the darkest time of his life thus far, ready to ask for their help in healing. Kit knew he did not deserve it.

What could have happened in six months? The biggest change would be the number of people in his family. His mother would have had the baby by now. Did he have a new brother or sister? Good Lord, he suddenly thought. What if something terrible had happened? Would they have written to him?

His father would have recovered from his surgery by now, he hoped well.

Lucy would have had her birthday, too. And Kit, being swept up in his new role, and forgotten to send her something.

He was lucky Emma did not have a birthday for a few months or he would have been royally punished by both his sisters.

Kit leaned his head back in the carriage for the last few moments of the ride. "Lord, I hope they forgive me," he whispered to himself. "I need them."

Kit opened the door once the carriage was stopped and instructed the driver to unload his trunk and then leave it. The footmen would collect it. Kit paid him handsomely for his services before walking up the steps to the door.

Kit took a deep breath. His movements were anticipated by Wade, their butler. The door was opened promptly and he was formally welcomed like a guest, and not a resident. Kit supposed that was fair.

"Welcome to Norwood, sir," he greeted formally, bowing his head.

Kit crossed the threshold into the house as two footmen exited to collect his trunk. "Hello there, Wade," murmured Kit. "Are my family here?"

No sooner had Kit had a chance to stand in the foyer and take in the surroundings that he had not seen for six months, Kit's question was answered, but not by Wade.

"They are," said a voice from above.

The hairs on Kit's neck suddenly stood up. Goose pimples covered his skin. Kit looked up to the landing that overlooked the foyer.

Daring to meet his father's eye, Kit suddenly felt like a fourteen year old boy again. When he first met Cassian, Kit felt so inferior, so stupid compared to this superior man who seemed to want an audience with him. Kit had felt ashamed of his own inferiorities.

Kit felt ashamed again. Not of his inferiorities, but for how he had handled the last six months.

Cassian's expression was hard. Unreadable. His black eyes betrayed nothing. He crossed his arms over his chest, standing rigidly.

There was no affection in the way that he looked down at Kit. There was no sense of him missing Kit, as Olivia had insisted when she had visited with him at Christmastime.

Cassian was still so angry at Kit. Kit knew that he had really hurt his father.

The footmen entered the house again, interrupting the staring going on between father and son. They went to carry the trunk up the stairs, but Cassian stopped them, holding his hand up.

"You are planning on staying?" he asked, emotionless.

Kit was suddenly fearful that things were so much worse than he feared. Was he not going to be allowed to stay? "Am I not welcome?" replied Kit.

"For God's sake, Cassian!" hissed his mother's voice. Kit could not see Faith, but in hearing her voice he knew she had to be standing in the hallway nearby.

"Let us go into the library." Cassian heeded his wife's words and began to descend the stairs. The footmen moved out of the way to accommodate him. "You may take that up to Master Kit's bedroom," he instructed them.

That brought Kit a little relief. Together, though silent, they walked into the Norwood library. It was much as he remembered it. Kit took a seat on one of the sofas while Cassian shut the door behind them. Cassian then joined him, choosing to sit opposite Kit.

Cassian still looked as hard as ever. His facial expression refused to betray any emotion to Kit. Kit, on the other hand, was certain he looked terrible. Weeks of sleepless nights would do that.

Kit knew he had just had to speak. He had to make peace. There had to be love between them again. It could not go on like this. "Father, I'm sorry," Kit said sincerely. "I am sorry for disappearing like I did. I am sorry for speaking to you the way I did. I disrespected you when I know that all you ever wanted was the best for me."

Kit would not ruin his apology with an excuse. He was glad of the result in running away. He had achieved something incredible. He was in a position to do such good in the world. He had made the right decision even if he had gone about it the wrong way.

And he had fallen in love. No matter how painful it felt right now.

Cassian exhaled and his jaw relaxed a little. "I never knew my father. I never had a man to guide me in the ways of the world, a father to fight for me, to be there for me, to provide for me. I knew that when I took you in I was going to give you the opportunities that I never had as a boy."

Cassian's tone was confusing to Kit. He did not sound angry, nor particularly happy. Was he accepting Kit's apology or just emphasising how ungrateful a son Kit was?

"I thought I knew what was best for you. And somewhere between teaching you to read and you walking out of this house I stopped listening to you. A monumental failure in my eyes."

The hard exterior of Cassian instantly melted away. Emotion filled his face. Kit could see the wretched longing suddenly in his father's eyes. Kit had been missed terribly.

"I pushed you," Cassian said, moving forward in his seat. "I pushed you into the life I wanted for you, and I did not stop to ask you what life you wanted for yourself. It took you leaving this house, leaving me, for me to realise that I was not the father I always thought I was."

"But the things I said ..." Kit chastised himself.

"The things you said to me were cruel," Cassian granted, showing the hurt in his eyes. "I do not think I will ever forget my son suggesting to me that I ought to have picked a more obedient orphan to be my son."

Kit winced. Had those words really come out of his mouth? Had he really wanted to injure his father that much in the moment? "Father, I'm sorry."

"I know you are," replied Cassian. "But after the initial shock had worn off, I got to thinking about your behaviour all these years we have been a family, and you were right. You have always done everything I have ever asked of you. You went to the schools I wanted. You left your teaching position when I asked. You helped with your sisters whenever we needed. You spent your holidays here instead of with your friends because I asked you to. And I got to thinking, what sort of father had I become that my own son could not tell me what he really wanted?"

"I never wanted to disappoint you."

"I know that now." Cassian smiled slightly.

"I never wanted to disappoint you because I was so proud to be your son. I am proud to be your son," Kit insisted. "You were never a terrible barbarian. You are the kindest man I know. You did everything for me and how did I thank you?"

Cassian sighed. He stood up from his sofa and joined Kit. "You do not need to thank me, Kit. We do not do the things we do as parents to receive thanks. We do it to see our children thrive, to see them have it better than we did. You will understand yourself when you are a parent one day." Cassian placed his hand on Kit's shoulder.

In feeling his father's hand, comforting as it was, Kit felt a significant weight life. His heart was still clouded with all that Olivia had done to it, but the pain was lighter now. "I want you to be proud of me, Father. Much has changed since I ... went away."

Cassian nodded. "Oh, my boy." He sighed. "There was never a prouder father than me as I watched you become an MP in January."

Kit was suddenly taken aback. "You were there?" he asked in disbelief.

Cassian nodded again. "I am sure I will quarrel horrendously with all of my children, but nothing will stop me from being present for their big moments. I am so proud of you, Kit, and I love you."

Kit pulled his father into a tight hug. "Forgive me," he willed.

Cassian chuckled and patted his back. "Of course, my boy." When they pulled apart, Cassian turned towards the door. "You can come in now!" he called.

The library door opened and Faith moved like lightning. Before Kit knew what was happening she was hugging him so tightly that he could not breathe. The first thing that Kit noticed about her was that she did not have a huge pregnant belly sticking into him. She had definitely had the baby.

"Mother!" coughed Kit.

Faith immediately released him and took a step back, though not releasing his hands. Faith looked so happy. As she had been the one writing him during his time away, Kit knew how much she had missed him.

"Mother, I am sorry for everything," Kit said sincerely.

Faith's brown eyes were watery. "I am just glad you are returned. It has not been the same with this hanging about the house." She wiped her eyes with her sleeve. "Where is Olivia? I expected the two of you to be together."

It was like a punch directly to the gut. Kit was saved from having to answer that question by a mop of curly black hair streaking into the library.

"Kit!" squealed Emma, stringing out the vowel sound in his name.

Kit caught her in his arms just as she jumped into them. Emma was so much bigger; he could not believe it. She was not even seven yet and she looked like a proper girl now, no longer little. Kit kissed her cheek. "I missed you, Emma."

"Don't ever go away again. I forget what you look like!" she cried dramatically.

"Well, I do have to go away in a little while," Kit told his sister, "but not just yet." Kit caught a glimpse of Lucy standing in the doorway of the library. She did not look as pleased to see Kit as Emma was. She also did not look so much as the Lucy he remembered. She was eleven now, and was turning into a young lady. She was no longer dressed as a little girl, with hems allowing her to run and play. She wore a proper gown with her brown hair braided just so. It was startling how grown up she was starting to look. "I missed you, Goose," Kit said to her.

Considering there was no blood relation, it was startling how similar Lucy's expression of displeasure was to Cassian's. "You missed Christmas!" she said accusingly. "And my birthday!"

Kit put Emma down on the floor. "I know," he said apologetically. "I am sorry. Can you forgive me?"

Lucy glared at him.

Kit threw himself on the floor dramatically. It was quite fun to play with his sisters again. It was nice to experience something light after the past few weeks of utter hell. "Please, Lucy!" Kit begged. "Please, forgive me!"

Lucy tried not the smile but she broke easily. She rolled her eyes and stalked over to Kit to give him a hug.

"I have a present for you," said Kit.

"Really?" Lucy asked excitedly in anticipation.

Kit produced the ring that he had presented to Olivia as an engagement ring. He had kept it in his pocket for the last month. He was torturing himself, really, by keeping it on his person. It ought to go to someone who would appreciate it.

"A grown up girl should have a grown up ring." Kit slipped the small ring onto Lucy's hand. It was a little big for her, but she would grow into it.

Lucy gasped with delight. "Mama!" she cried. "Mama, look at my present!" She rushed over to Faith to show off her ring.

Both Cassian and Faith exchanged a glance. Kit knew that they knew exactly what that ring had been, and who it had been intended for. He could see on their faces that they had begun to piece together what might have happened.

The ring, Olivia's absence, and the fact that Kit looked absolutely dreadful, all had to mean that something had happened. Kit would tell them about it when he was ready.

He was glad that they seemed to understand this instead of pressing for information.

"Kit," said Faith, a smile forming on her face. "How would you like to be introduced to your brother?"

Chapter 24

K it was relieved at the feeling of joy that filled him when he learned he had a brother. It was such a pleasant change from the despair that had taken up residence in his heart these last weeks.

"He came February seventh," Cassian informed him, "as an early birthday gift for Lucy."

"And all is well?" Kit asked his mother, concern in his tone.

Faith nodded. "All is well," she assured him. "He is healthy. I am healthy. I did not want to inform you in a letter," she added tentatively. "I wanted for us all to be together."

"I understand," Kit replied. "In fact, I am glad I can be here to meet him. Please, introduce me," he urged.

Cassian proudly led the family out of the library. Faith walked beside Kit and the girls followed behind.

"He is very excited to have an infant son," Faith whispered to Kit. "But I do not want you to worry. You will always be his eldest."

Kit had not been worrying. In fact, he was in suddenly realisation of something. This boy was Cassian's blood son. His heir. Legally, this boy would be in receipt of everything. He would be responsible for Lucy and Emma, if they were not married, upon his inheritance. It was an odd feeling knowing that an infant, twenty-two years his junior, was to be responsible for his sisters.

As it had been with Emma, the baby was not kept in a nursery, but in a bassinet in his parent's bedroom. The bassinet was a gorgeous white, wicker bed draped with gossamer fabric.

Lucy and Emma trotted over to the bed, peeking inside. Kit followed carefully being led by his parents. In seeing the four of them surrounding the bassinet, Kit felt such a sense of home. No matter what happened in the future, he could not make the same mistake by walking out on his family again. These people, his people, were far too precious to him.

And there was now one more to love.

Kit peered inside the bassinet. The baby, his brother, was sleeping. He looked so peaceful, unaffected by how cruel the world could be sometimes. Kit got down on his knees so we was looking in at the same height as Lucy. He reached in carefully and stroked his brother's cheeks. It had been a long time since he had felt the softness of a baby's skin. In fact, Emma had been the last baby he had held. It would never cease to amaze him how smooth they were.

He was wrapped in white bedclothes, and a small cap was keeping his head warm, but Kit could see little tufts of dark hair poking out from underneath it. His eyelashes were dark as well. He had definitely inherited Cassian's dark features.

This dear child was so innocent. Heir or not, this boy was another one of Kit's younger siblings. He would always be responsible for him, and he would be glad to guide him.

"What is he called?" asked Kit softly.

"Tom," said Cassian proudly. "Thomas Sky Kensington is what he will be christened."

The significance of his second name did not escape Kit. It honoured his mother's first born son, the child she had lost.

"A good, strong name," Kit decided. "Welcome to the world, young Tom."

"I am so happy you are home, Kit," Faith said quietly.

Kit met his mother's eyes and saw that they were glassy. "Mother, don't cry."

"I cannot help it. I have wished for this sight before me for so long and I am so happy that is has finally come to fruition. I do not ever want us to argue like that again. Any issue that arises will be discussed calmly and rationally," she said firmly, yet emotionally.

"I agree," nodded Cassian.

"You have my word," Kit promised.

They spent the next hour fussing over the baby. The noise around young Tom stirred him, and once he was awake and settled, Kit had a turn holding him. Kit gently rocked his brother, and marvelled yet again how perfect and innocent he was.

This young man would have a lot to offer a young lady one day. Kit doubted he would ever be abandoned.

When Tom tired again, Faith put him back down in the bassinet and Lucy and Emma kept watch over him.

Kit, Cassian and Faith then went to sit down on the settees in front of the fireplace.

"Now, I am sure the thought has crossed your mind," Cassian began. "What will happen when I die?"

Kit scoffed. "No, Father, I cannot say that I spend a lot of time thinking about your death."

"You know what I mean." Cassian shook his head at Kit's sarcasm. "You know the law. Tom is my heir now, and I want you to know what that means for you."

"As I said, nothing has changed. You are still the eldest," Faith interjected. "You are still their older brother," she said, nodding to the younger three.

"Exactly," agreed Cassian. "Now, you legally own half of this estate and all the income it generates. I made sure of that when I purchased it that your name was on the deed of purchase, just as I will if and when I purchase any other holdings. When I die, Tom will inherit my half of this estate, as well as the factories and the money. You know how it can be. I could die of fever tomorrow and Tom would still be an infant. You are a man, and I need to rely on you to take care of your mother and siblings."

It was if they were asking him to burden himself. Kit frowned. "I will endeavour to be a better brother to all three of them then I have been these last months," he promised. "I am grateful that you took measures to ensure my future when you purchased this estate, Father, but I assure you that I do not resent Tom his rightful inheritance."

Faith took Kit's hand and squeezed it. "Tom is so uniquely blessed to have an older brother to guide him towards his future. We obviously understand you have such important responsibilities in London now, but we hope that you will visit and stay when the opportunities present themselves." She paused. "That is, of course, if you are not otherwise ... engaged?"

Kit knew that his mother had not used that word in the context of marriage but it still stung just the same. He had not hid his reaction from his parents well.

"Kit, what happened? You look terrible," Cassian stated.

"You are too kind," retorted Kit.

Faith shuffled closed to Kit on the sofa and put her arm around him comfortingly. "You know what he means," she said softly. "But you do look really tired." She was putting it kindly. "The ring you gave to Lucy ..." she trailed off.

"Is it an engagement ring, son?" asked Cassian.

"It was," he confirmed. He coughed trying to suppress the humiliating sobs that wanted to come. "I know you do not approve, Father, but it turned out she didn't want the ring anyway."

"What?" gasped Faith.

"She turned you down?" Cassian asked in disbelief.

"Well, I never got a chance to ask. She did not like where her life was heading with me, and so she left to ... change the world." It sounded like an exaggeration but Kit was fully confident in Olivia's ability to lobby and work for whatever she set her mind to.

"Oh, I am so sorry, Kit!" Faith said sympathetically. "But I could have sworn when she visited us at Christmas that there would have been a different outcome. We both thought so."

"I might not like her family, Kit, but I do approve of her. She came to tell me of the election date, to ask me to come. When we spoke at the election she so desperately wanted us to talk. The way she cared for you made me really think that ..." Cassian stopped, probably when he realised the dry glare that Kit was giving him. "I am sorry for you, Kit," he said sincerely.

"But you mustn't give up hope!" insisted Faith. "Have hope that she will see sense!"

"But she is seeing sense," replied Kit. "I may not like her decision at the moment but she has gone to do exactly what she has been trying to do since the moment I met her. She is trying to make the world better."

Faith smiled sadly. "Well, have hope that you both will find happiness, together or apart. I want you both to be happy."

"I am happy being here with you all," Kit responded.

No matter that he still felt the constant ache of daggers in his chest, he felt the smallest ounce of optimism. There could be happiness again.

Chapter 25

September, 1824

Nine Years Later

It still felt a little odd to Olivia at times when she sat in what was once her grandfather's study. She could still picture him at times smoking his cigars, reading the paper, and being quite oblivious to what was going on around him.

It was her office now. It had been since her grandfather had passed away the winter following her leaving London. Olivia and her aunt grieved for Bernard Murray deeply, but his death set in motion a series of events that Olivia felt so fortunate for.

Upon Bernard's death, Olivia's Uncle Colin, and Bernard's only son, inherited the baronetcy and the estate. Colin, however, was settled with his family in Surrey, and his wife did not want to leave.

There was now the matter of the house. What was to happen to it? Who was to live in it? Would it be sold?

Olivia had not the income to lease it from her uncle, and Lorna's obligations were now elsewhere. It was not until Ruth had arrived at the Murray estate one evening with a lifeline that Olivia would be forever grateful for.

Ruth gifted Olivia a cheque for twenty-five thousand pounds, her dowry, minus the bits and pieces she had taken from it throughout her childhood to fund teachers and schools.

"I now know it is highly unlikely your father and I will ever put this money into the hands of your husband." It was Ruth's backhanded way of accepting that Olivia would not be marrying any time soon.

Olivia had left London to do what she had always intended. To change the world. A lofty ambition at the best of times. All she had managed to do between leaving London and her grandfather passing was stock libraries, pay a few teaching wages, and offer tutoring.

She now had twenty-five thousand pounds to achieve her goal.

And she had achieved it.

Olivia now sat in her own office, the office of the founder of the Women's College of Knowledge and Improvement. Using the money, she had leased the estate from her uncle, and had founded the school.

It was not a finishing school. It was a school where girls could seek the same further education that men could at the most prestigious universities in the country.

Once girls had finished their schooling in their own villages, they could come to Olivia's college to study and further their abilities to give them greater opportunities than merely marrying for security.

She had started off with only a handful of pupils, and one teacher: herself.

Olivia's school was condemned. It was not a woman's place to learn. She needed to marry and procreate. There was a reason only men were permitted to attend university.

It only further fuelled Olivia's desire to succeed.

Olivia brought in like-minded teachers to school the girls on subjects like science and philosophy. It was Olivia's desire to give women education and training, safety essentially from needing to marry, as opposed to wanting to marry.

Olivia's school was in its eighth year of operation. In that time, the school had produced writers, mathematicians, teachers, nurses, midwives, thinkers, people that could contribute more to society than being a mere domestic servant to her family.

Olivia's next goal? To have a doctor graduate from her school. She knew it would take a lot of fighting, but if anyone had the ambition, it was her.

The nurses and midwives that were already being trained at the college practically had the knowledge of a doctor, they just could not be called so. In the meantime, Olivia was glad that she was able to train women who could provide safe and informed care to others regardless of their title.

Olivia received letters often from students past.

Nothing made her prouder than hearing from a former pupil who was supporting her family through work gained from her own ability. There would always be challenges in securing work as a woman, but Olivia used her influence wherever she could to help her pupils.

She had a knack for digging in her heels until she got her way.

Olivia received applications from both men and woman every day. Olivia accommodated all she could, but she was limited for space at the Murray estate. She taught and housed two hundred pupils at a time. Two dozen of the upstairs rooms had been converted into bunkrooms and the majority of the downstairs rooms had been converted into classrooms,

Tuition was subject to circumstance. Olivia charged the vast majority of the students a pound a month for board and schooling. This income helped her to pay her teachers and keep the school running smoothly.

When she received applications from men, the turnover of the school allowed her to sponsor those she could to institutions that admitted men. Olivia had helped men who would have otherwise been factory workers, to study medicine and law among other subjects. Her greatest success was a man named John Belby, the son of a farmer who became a solicitor and was now the apprentice of the Lord Chief Justice in London. Her uncle had sponsored his admittance at Olivia's insistence.

Olivia knew that she was not a conventional woman of the time. She knew that many people disliked her, hated her even, and hated what she stood for even more. But she was proud of herself. Olivia never could have been happy with her life if she had simply stood by and watched others do the work. She wanted to get her hands dirty.

And now, sitting in her own office, surrounded by letters of testimony as to the positive effect that she had had on the lives of hundreds of women, and the lives of men too, she was satisfied that she had changed the world, even if it was only her little corner of it.

Olivia sifted through the mail that had been delivered that morning and pounced on the letter from her aunt when she saw Lorna's handwriting. Even though Lorna lived in a neighbouring village, they still corresponded twice, sometimes thrice weekly.

Lorna had been very supportive of Olivia's idea to turn Bernard Murray's house into a school. She had not wanted the estate to be sold and was glad that it could be saved. Lorna had stayed with her beloved father until the end, and had only revealed her attachment to her fiancé after Bernard's death. Olivia had always known that her aunt would never leave her father.

Strangely, Olivia was not surprised to learn that while she had been away nine years earlier that Lorna had formed an attachment to the magistrate who had arrested her for voting in the Norwood election. She had detected a flirtation at the time but had not given it any more thought until Lorna revealed the engagement.

Finn Kelly and Lorna's wedding a few months later had been the last time that Olivia had seen the Kensingtons, although the eldest son had been absent from the nuptials. It was too difficult for both parties to maintain the relationship.

But Finn and Lorna had been living happily ever since, and Olivia enjoyed doting on their six year old son Patrick, her cousin, often.

Olivia read Lorna's letter, thanking her for Paddy's birthday present and inviting her for dinner the following week once Olivia was returned from London.

Just as Olivia was about to pen her reply to Lorna, there was a knock on her door.

"Come in," called Olivia.

The door opened and the butler, Stoughton entered. "Pardon the interruption, milady, but you have a visitor. A potential pupil."

"Oh, well let her in then," encouraged Olivia. She stood up from the desk and watched as Stoughton made way for her visitor.

She was a young woman. She looked to be about twenty or so, with a fair face. She was very pretty indeed, with dark brown hair fixed elegantly and dark brown eyes. She was dressed very richly, wearing a gown the colour of corn silk adorned with expensive lace. She was not the sort of girl that Olivia was used to receiving, but Olivia was willing to help anyone who sought to better themselves.

As she walked nervously towards Olivia, something about her seemed familiar. Olivia walked around the desk and extended her hand to her guest. She only hesitated slightly before shaking Olivia's hand.

"I know, it seems strange. You get into the habit of it though. I refuse to have my hand kissed by a man. I have no desire for his spit on my skin, thank you very much," Olivia joked, hoping to ease the girl's nerves.

It seemed to work as she laughed.

"My name is Olivia Pendleton," she introduced herself, offering the girl a seat. "Please sit down. What is your name?"

"Yes, I know who you are. We have met before," replied the girl as she took the seat Olivia offered.

Olivia knew that she had seemed familiar. "Pray, tell me who you are."

"My name is Lucy Kensington," she replied.

Olivia could not help but open her mouth in surprise. Of course it was Lucy. She could see it now. How remarkably similar she was to her mother, Olivia's aunt. "Of course you are," Olivia said after a moment of shock. "Lucy, how are you?"

Lucy smiled, albeit the nerves still present in her demeanour. "I am well," she replied.

"Lucy, what can I do for you?"

Lucy bit her bottom lip before saying, "I am in need of guidance, I suppose. I was hoping you could help me."

"I shall try."

Lucy huffed with embarrassment. "I shall not dance around the subject. You know I am illegitimate. Everyone knows I am illegitimate. My position in life does not reflect my family's."

It was indeed unfortunate how well circulated the circumstances of Lucy Kensington's birth was. It did not matter that she had a good, respectable surname. She was illegitimate and there would always be those who would turn their noses up at her because of it.

Lucy seemed so uncomfortable and embarrassed at saying such things to Olivia. She seemed to channel her nervous energy into fiddling with a ring that she wore on her right hand.

Olivia had to do a double take when she saw the ring. It, like Lucy, she had seen before. The gold band with emerald stones had been presented to her. That ring had been Olivia's engagement ring.

Olivia sucked in a breath as her heart rate started to pick up. It was as if reality had suddenly landed on her shoulders, nine years of denial rearing its ugly head. She had done her best not to think about him for the best part of a decade. She couldn't think about him. Thinking about him would distract her from her vision, from her ambition.

And yet here he was, on Lucy Kensington's finger, staring at her with his bright green eyes. That vision was almost starling. She could still remember the exact hue of his eyes.

"Are you alright, Miss Pendleton? You look awfully pale."

Olivia snapped out of her panic and did her best to focus on Lucy. "Yes, I am fine," she said, lying through her teeth. "Please, go on."

Lucy nodded. "Well, I am afraid that I will never get married. Nobody will ever marry me, and anybody who would marry me would be doing so for the wrong reasons." Olivia could see the genuine fear in Lucy's eyes. It was a fear that Olivia hated. Women felt such a responsibility to be married.

Olivia had many philosophies, but her philosophy on marriage was one that she spoke of the most. "I am afraid I cannot help you find a husband," replied Olivia, "but I can help you not to need one."

"That is what I want," confirmed Lucy. "I want to learn how to support myself. I know my parents would never resent me, but I never want to become a burden to them."

Olivia could tell that Lucy was not at the college for education. She was not hungry for further study as her other pupils were. She was afraid, and rightly so. Olivia hated to think of the abuse that Lucy had experienced from others. People could be terribly cruel. Olivia wagered that at her age, her friends were getting married and were leaving her behind, and Lucy was afraid of what was to happen to her.

In knowing the characters of her aunt and her husband, they would have raised Lucy as though she was no different to her siblings. And yet Lucy was different. She was not prepared for life beyond the walls of Norwood Cottage and she was afraid.

"Lucy, I understand more than most what it is to be vilified for who you are. My school is a place where women can come to seek equal opportunity in education. What you need, I feel, is a friend to tell you that everything will be alright."

Olivia could tell that she had hit a nerve. Lucy looked more vulnerable than ever.

"But no one will ever marry me," she stated fearfully.

Olivia smiled sympathetically. "There is someone out there for everyone." Spying that ring on Lucy's finger reminded Olivia that there had once been someone for her as well. "Marriage is not something that should be entered into because it is fashionable, or because you are afraid of being called a spinster. I am eight and twenty years old! I have heard the name calling but I do not let it influence my conviction. It is not something to be rushed into when you are still a girl. It is not something that should be entered into with thoughts of money or security. You should not marry merely to be married. Women ought to use their right to choose a husband for the right reasons. You must take the time to seek answers from your proposed spouse. Does he love you? Does he support you? Does he listen to you? Does he believe in you? And this one I am particularly passionate about. Does he advocate for you?" Olivia exhaled. "Why chain yourself for life to a man who could not answer yes to all those questions?"

Lucy seemed to sit back in her chair and ponder Olivia's words. It was a speech Olivia had given many times before. Marriage for convenience was one of the practices she was endeavouring to stop through education. If women could earn their own wage, they would not have the need to marry so quickly. They would have the luxury to choose a husband later, one whom they had properly gotten to know.

"I do understand the point you are trying to make," replied Lucy after a while, "but my fear is that no one will ever want to marry me. Who would tie themselves to someone like me?" Lucy was becoming quite emotional at the thought.

Olivia was quickly out of her chair again and offering Lucy a handkerchief. "The right man will," she promised. "The right man will not care a wit about your birth. He will love every part of you."

Lucy accepted the handkerchief and wiped her eyes. "Thank you," she said gratefully. "I hope you are right."

"I am never wrong," she retorted confidently.

"Do you think you will ever get married?" Lucy asked. "If you find a man who could answer yes to all your questions?"

Olivia looked down at Lucy's ring, she hoped nonchalantly. "I almost did," she replied honestly, "to a man who loved and supported me beyond anything." Lucy's ignorance of this hurt Olivia in a way. She had no knowledge of her past with Kit, which had to mean that Kit had never mentioned her.

Of course he hadn't. He had gifted Olivia's engagement ring to his sister! Kit had left Olivia in his past. Olivia could not fathom how that fact was affecting her.

"Why didn't you marry him?" Lucy asked curiously.

Why didn't Olivia marry Kit? What had stopped her? She had been nineteen for starters. She felt that she had so much more to do with her life than be a politician's wife. She hadn't achieved any of her goals. It didn't make sense for someone like her to be married, to belong to a man and to lose her independence.

Standing here as a mature woman, she could argue against each and every one of those points. But at the time, she had felt that she needed to leave to reach her goals. Look at what she had achieved because of it.

She was helping girls, teaching them, coaching them on all sorts, including marriage, and she had never taken her own advice.

Nine years earlier, sitting on that bench, she could have answered yes to every one of her questions. Had she stayed, had she sat and talked to Kit, allowed him to understand properly what she was going through, she could have still achieved her dreams. Kit was not the sort of man to keep her in the house, expecting her to make social calls on with wives of other MPs. How could she have ever thought that would have been her life?

Olivia shook off the doubts. It would not help anything now. It was in the past. It was done. She would never see Kit again. She had not all this time, so what benefit was there thinking about this? "Because at the time, I believed that what I wanted to achieve in my life did not correspond with being married," replied Olivia.

Lucy did not press the issue further. She stood up from her chair and faced Olivia. "I am really grateful that you took the time to speak to me," she said sincerely. "You are living proof, I think, that not every woman needs to be married to be happy."

"You are welcome, Lucy. Let me see you out, and then I ought to organise myself. I am away to London tomorrow. Scouting a new building for a second school. I want to take on more pupils, we have just run out of room here." Olivia smiled, albeit not as wide as she usually did. Not every woman needed to be married to be happy. But was it possible that Olivia might have been happy with the right man? She was satisfied with her life, but was she happy?

Epilogue

"Today I am very proud of the house," Kit said powerfully, standing at the front bench beside Prime Minister Ashcroft. "That we could come together to not only invest in the future of this country, but to ensure the immediate futures of our children."

It was difficult for Kit to maintain his firm, unwavering demeanour. Today was a day that he had been working towards for years. Two thirds of the house had just passed a bill making schooling compulsory for girls to the age of fifteen and boys to the age of thirteen. This was Kit's law. This was what he had entered parliament to do.

It was at times like these that there was really only one person that Kit would like to celebrate with. But he never opened that door. He closed it a long time ago, along with it the pain.

"Now as we conclude this session of parliament, I would ask you all to join with me in saying a prayer and sending our deepest condolences to His Majesty on the passing of the Prince of Wales, and we ask for the protection and guidance of our new Prince of Wales."

Kit led the house in a heartfelt prayer. Politicians and the Royals alike were never meant to show an affinity for the other, but the death of the Prince of Wales had quickly shocked London, and would the rest of the nation when the news spread to the papers outside the city.

Charles had fallen from his horse only yesterday, and his death had been swift. Kit had not known the prince well, only that his father loved him dearly, and would be deeply hurt by his loss. Kit felt more for Edward, his greatest, though secret, friend. Edward was now the Prince of Wales, the future King. Kit had not the opportunity to see his friend, though if he knew Edward, he would have gotten himself as far away from London as possible. This sudden pressure, coupled with his father's disapproval of him, would kill him.

"Well said, Kensington," commended the PM upon the parliament's closing.

Kit smiled. "Thank you, sir. I am sorry for the Royal Family."

"Yes, yes, we all are," Mr Ashcroft said dismissively. "It is not as though there is a succession crisis though. What I was talking about was your bill. Excellently said, excellently put, an all-around good job." He slapped Kit on the back.

Mr Ashcroft had been Kit's mentor these last nine years. He had helped Kit rise through the ranks, so that he was now his number two as Ashcroft was PM. But upon the next election in only a month, the aging Mr Ashcroft was to stand down, and Kit, the once illiterate orphan without a name, was to stand as Prime Minister.

Despite the turmoil he knew that his friend would be feeling at this moment, Kit could not wipe the smile off of his face as he left parliament. He had really accomplished something today. The country would be a better place after today. Children would be educated for longer, given better opportunities than their parents.

Poverty, Kit hoped, would one day be a thing of the past.

Kit climbed into his carriage and he was taken directly to his father's house in Kensington. Kit lived there mainly at his mother's insistence. She was convinced it was safer then the rooms he had been renting. Despite thinking her paranoid, he could not deny that he enjoyed the space.

Kit unlocked the gate and went inside the house. He kept a very minimal staff as he paid them out of his own pocket. A housekeeper, a cook, and a driver only. Kit could dress himself and he could answer his own door, so he had no need for a butler or a manservant.

Kit thought first to check his mail for news from Edward. It was highly likely he would have fled to a brothel in France to drown his sorrows and he would have written to tell his only friend where he was going. Kit jogged up the stairs and went into his study. Sure enough, the mail had been left on his desk for him. Kit went directly over to the desk and collected the letters, flipping through them to find Edward's.

One from his mother. One from Lucy. One from Emma. One from Tom, though poorly addressed in his childish hand. But none from Edward.

"I thought I would bring it myself," a dull voice sounded from the corner.

Kit spun around, startled, to see that Edward was crouched in the corner of the study, his head between his knees. In his hand was a letter.

Edward looked dreadful. His eyes were red, from crying or from lack of sleep. His hair and clothing were dishevelled and Kit could now pick up the scent of whiskey. How had he managed to get in the house? The gate had been locked. Had he scaled the gate? Kit was certain Faith would be very happy to know the house was not impervious to intruders.

"Oh, my friend," Kit said sympathetically. "I am so terribly sorry."

"So am I," he replied bluntly. "He falls from a bloody horse and dies. How does that happen? People fall off of horses all the time and they are fine. My brother falls and suddenly I am next in line."

Kit walked over to Edward carefully. "Edward, you mustn't panic about such things now. It is a time to mourn, a time to grieve. When is the funeral?"

Kit could see the anxiety in Edward's fearful blue eyes. "Do you want to know what he said to me when Charles died?" he asked, his voice breaking. "He said, 'Better it had been you'"

Kit sucked in a breath in shock. "He can't have meant that."

"But he did," insisted Edward. "Charles was the perfect son. He was the one who was meant to be king. My father would rather have me dead then take the place of Charles." Edward sniffed as he started to cry, wiping his eyes on his very expensive sleeves.

"Your father is upset," Kit offered quietly. "He has lost his son. When the funeral is over and the grief passes I am sure things will be different." Kit was not certain that he believed his own words. In the decade or so that Kit had known Edward, he had not known Edward's father to offer him a single word of kindness.

"I am not going to the funeral," Edward said with determination. "I am going to France." Kit had been right about the destination. "I cannot pray and mourn over my brother's coffin with my father standing beside him wishing it were me that was inside it."

Kit did not have an argument for that. But he did know of a safer place then France for his friend to hide for a while. "I am going to organise a bath for you," to get rid of the whiskey smell, "and then I am going to take you to Norwood. You can stay there as long as you like."

Edward sniffed as he started to cry, wiping his eyes on his very expensive sleeves.

And perhaps Edward would feel capable of ruling an empire after being around Kit's family for a little while. Their support had given Kit all the confidence in the world.

While Edward was in the bath, Kit wrote his apologies, excusing himself from parliament for the next week or so, citing a family emergency. Edward was like a brother to him after all. Kit organised some clothing to take with him and decided on some items to lend to Edward. Kit was taller than his friend so he would have to tuck his breeches into his boots.

Only an hour or so later, they were both in the carriage on their way to Derbyshire. They stopped only to change horses and to allow the driver to rest. They made excellent time and found themselves travelling through the gates of Norwood Cottage two and a half days later.

Now that Edward was clean and sober, he was functioning a little more rationally. He had not cried, though Kit was unsure if that was a good thing or not, seeing as his own brother had only been dead a few days.

"Are you sure your family won't mind my intrusion?" Edward asked quietly as the carriage pulled to a stop.

"Not at all," Kit promised.

They climbed out of the carriage and were quickly met by his father's servants. Kit gave them instructions before leading Edward into the house. Edward had not been to Kit's house for several years. In fact, Kit could not recall the last time. It was not often that Edward's father allowed cross-country trips.

Kit's mother was the first to greet them. She appeared from the drawing room and excitedly hugged Kit in greeting.

"We were not expecting you!" cried Faith, before she turned to see that Kit had brought along a royal guest. "Oh my, Kit you might have warned me. Your Royal Highness," she curtseyed respectfully. Both Faith and Cassian were acquainted with Edward properly after having visited Kit in London last year, but his siblings had not met with him in several years.

"I am sorry to trespass on your hospitality, Mrs Kensington," Edward said regretfully. "I took Kit unawares as well. I do not know if the news has reached you yet."

"What news?" Faith asked, alarmed. Cassian had just emerged from somewhere as well, and joined the gathering in the foyer. He immediately sensed the tension and did not offer his son more than a smile in greeting.

Kit watched as Edward turned his face, the words getting stuck in his throat. "The Prince of Wales was killed in an accident on Thursday," Kit said softly.

Faith gasped and Cassian's expression dropped.

"Oh, God," swore Cassian. "Your Royal Highness, you have our deepest condolences."

Edward regained some of his composure and offered Kit's parents a grimace-like smile. "Thank you."

"Come and sit down," urged Faith, directing them all towards the drawing room. "I shall ring for some tea. Cassian, go and fetch Emma and Tom."

"Where is Lucy?" Kit asked.

"Oh, she should be home soon. She is out with Violet today," replied Faith.

Wade delivered afternoon refreshments and Kit's siblings joined the gathering in the drawing room.

Sixteen year old Emma sat beside Faith on the settee, and nine year old Tom beside Cassian. Both favoured Cassian greatly, sharing his dark curly hair and charcoal eyes. Though luckily, Emma's features were soft and feminine, like Faith's. It had only been four weeks or so since Kit had last seen Tom but he was already growing like a weed. It would only be a few short years before he would be away to school.

Kit's family tried their best to make cheerful conversation with Edward while Edward acquainted himself with Kit's younger siblings. Edward had never met Tom, and Emma had only been small when she had last met the prince.

Already Kit saw a sense of relaxation in his friend. How could Edward possibly handle his grief when his father was so venomous in his?

"Oh, I did not realise we had company," cried Lucy, who had entered the drawing room unbuttoning her coat. She froze when she realised who their guest was.

"Edward, you remember my sister, Lucy, don't you?" introduced Kit. "She was smaller when you knew her last."

Edward looked over to the doorway and his eyes widened. He immediately rose to his feet and bowed his head at Lucy before she had a chance to curtsey to him. "You have only grown more beautiful in age, my lady."

Kit immediately exchanged a look with his father. Was Edward taken with Lucy? Kit knew that Lucy was very pretty. She had inherited their mother's beauty. But Edward couldn't be taken with Lucy. Such a connection was quite impossible for reasons that seemed to consistently embarrass and limit Kit's sister.

Lucy's cheeks reddened. "Oh, well, thank you," she stammered, managing to clumsily curtsey. "It is a pleasure to make your acquaintance again, Your Royal Highness."

"The pleasure is all mine." Edward had not broken eye contact with Lucy and all in the drawing room were very aware of it. Were Edward not a prince, Kit was certain his father would have knocked him out for staring at Lucy so.

Lucy seemed to be terribly self-conscious at the attention. Attention, at least positive attention was not something she was used to. Lucy was used to abrasiveness and snide comments. She had certainly not been on the receiving end of a gentleman's attention before now.

"Emma, would you play for us?" Faith almost shouted, cutting the awkwardness in the room.

Emma quickly scurried over to the pianoforte and began to play a tune. Attention turned to her, at which time Kit rose from his seat and went over to meet Lucy.

Kit loved all his siblings, but he had a particular affection for Lucy. She had the same privileged upbringing, but the prejudice she endured was like nothing else, especially in such a little village. Kit felt very protective over her, and she was the one he regretted being parted from the most when he was away in London.

"Where were you today?" he asked her.

"I was with Violet," she replied.

"Seeing as I saw and spoke to Violet on Piccadilly Circus the other day, and she informed me of the length of her stay in London, would you like to try again?"

Lucy looked down guiltily. "Alright, alright, I visited the Women's College today," she confessed.

Kit felt the blood leaving his face.

"I spoke with Olivia Pendleton," continued Lucy. "She runs the college, you know."

Kit did know. What Lucy and his siblings were unaware of was Kit's previous attachment to Olivia.

Kit knew all about Olivia's college. It was a frequent cause of scandal in the newspapers, although the outrage had died down in recent years. It had not surprised Kit at all that Olivia had founded a school, a college, for women. She had been determined to change the world and she had found an extraordinary way to do it.

Kit had been angry in the beginning. He would have supported her in founding her school. He would have helped her. But as he grew up and matured over the years, he could only be proud of her.

The hurt, and the love, was still there. It always would be, Kit was certain. After nine years and still feeling such love towards another person, Kit was absolutely certain it would never go away. That was why he locked it away and tried not to feel it. Love was supposed to be wonderful. But it only could be when it was reciprocated.

"W-why did you speak with Olivia?"

"I wanted to speak to her about attending her school," replied Lucy nonchalantly.

It was an incredible thing to suddenly comprehend. His sister had been in the same room as Olivia today. She had conversed with her as if it were something that happened every day. Had Olivia's thoughts gone to him when she had spoken with Lucy? Had she thought of him at all? Had he even entered her mind these last nine years?

"She helped me to realise that I was not there to seek further education. I am lucky that Mama and Papa secured a well-rounded education for me. I suppose I was afraid that my position would prevent me from ever marrying. But she helped me to see that the right man will love me, support me, listen to me, believe in me, and he will advocate for me. It is a rule she has. Why chain ourselves to someone for life if he does not do those things?"

Kit could hear Olivia's voice in Lucy's words. It was startling to know that he could still recall her pitch and tone after so long. But those words, didn't she know that she already had that herself? "Indeed," Kit managed to say. "And has she found such a man?"

Kit had not heard that she was married. But if Lucy answered yes to this question he was sure he would need some help to remain standing.

"She did," replied Lucy. "She told me that she almost married a man that loved and supported her beyond anything, but that she couldn't go through with it because being married and going about her goals didn't correlate."

Olivia was talking about Kit. She had to be talking about him. Kit had loved her more than words. And that was the excuse she had given him when she had left him all those years ago. She needed to go out into the world and achieve her dreams. She had done that.

"I think she still loves him though, which is so terribly sad," Lucy continued.

Kit's attention suddenly snapped back to his sister. "What makes you say that?"

"Her expression when she spoke of him. The way she looked told me that he was still so important to her. But they are obviously apart, which is sad."

Could it really be so? After all this time, could Olivia still feel some regard for him? Could she feel love for him?

The thought made him feel sick. He had suffered a heartbreaking rejection once before. How could he endure such a thing again? How could he even entertain being in that position again?

"Because I love her," Kit whispered to himself.

"What?" asked Lucy.

"Nothing," Kit retorted quickly. "I am glad Miss Pendleton helped you to find some clarity, Lucy. You know how much we detest the way people vilify you."

Lucy actually laughed. "That is the word Olivia used to describe it. But now I have to find something to do with myself. I am twenty now. Violet is in London buying wedding clothes. She was my only friend here."

"Pardon my interruption." Edward was suddenly beside them.

Kit checked behind him to see his parents and Tom still watching Emma at the pianoforte.

"Not at all Your Royal Highness," Lucy curtseyed again.

Edward's eyes looked over Lucy fondly. Kit did not feel at all comfortable with his friend's sudden attraction. He was in a terrible state of grief, and he was not thinking clearly. Lucy would not be his plaything.

Lucy, however, seemed innocent, or oblivious, to the attention she was receiving in that moment.

"My sister, Alice, is in need of another lady-in-waiting. You would be her attendant at court, accompany her, and be her friend. You would not know a better friend than my sister. I adore her. And if you are looking to leave Derbyshire, I can promise you that London can be a wonderful distraction from the woes of life."

Kit had not been expecting that. Edward was offering Lucy a place at court. She would be in attendance to Princess Alice. That was an incredible honour. The most Kit could want for Lucy. But, there was one obvious hindrance to this plan.

Lucy seemed to realise this, too. "That is incredibly kind of you, sir," she said gratefully, "and I know what an honour it is to be asked. But I cannot accept. Surely you know what I am." Lucy's cheeks flushed red as she looked away from Edward.

"I only want good, kind people around my sister. With the way your brother speaks of you, I know all I need to," replied Edward confidently. "Besides, I am sure that parliament will not object to the new Prime Minister's sister at court. In fact, I think they would look at it as an advantage to them."

Kit could see the excitement building in his sister's brown eyes. This would be good for her. This would give her confidence and, Kit prayed, a level of respect and acceptance.

"Well, I would have to ask my parents first." Lucy smiled widely. Her smile made Edward smile, and it was the happiest Kit had seen his friend look all week.

Kit could not see how this could end in anything but tears.

"Don't you have somewhere to be?" Edward challenged Kit, raising his eyebrows.

"What are you talking about?"

"I was eavesdropping on your conversation. Isn't there a certain redhead that you ought to be chasing right about now?"

"What are you both talking about?" asked Lucy.

Kit exhaled, smiling. "Yes, I think there is. Pray for me. I will go to her directly." God help him.

"Olivia?" gasped Lucy in realisation. The reality seemed to dawn on her immediately. "She was talking about you! Oh, Kit, you ought to hurry! She told me she was leaving for London soon, off to scout another location for her school!"

"Thank you, Goose. Tell Mother and Father where I have gone," Kit instructed, kissing his sister's forehead. "Goodbye!" he shouted over his shoulder as he ran from the drawing room, hearing the sudden confusion of his family as he ran into the September air.

Kit had never saddled a horse faster in his life, and was away to Olivia's school within minutes, it felt like.

As he rode, Kit's heart beating out of his chest, Kit put behind him all fear, all hesitation. He could not be afraid. He had to trust that the years had been good to them both. They were older now, more mature, more prepared to take on the world together.

When Kit reached Olivia's school, he leapt of his horse and ran up to her door. Lord, he was certain her looked dreadful. He used his handkerchief to wipe the sweat from his brow and attempted to comb his hair with his fingers right up until the door was opened for him.

Kit recognised the butler, Stoughton, but he was not certain if he recognised Kit.

He looked at him with a quizzical expression. "Yes?"

"I seek an audience with Miss Pendleton ... please," Kit stammered nervously.

"Do you have an appointment? The mistress has already been disturbed enough today," he said stiffly.

"No, I don't," confessed Kit, "but I am an old friend. She will want to see me." At least Kit hoped she would.

"Your name?"

"Kit Kensington," Kit replied. This would prove whether or not she wanted to see him.

Stoughton seemed to recognise his name and he invited Kit inside the house. "Very well, I will tell the mistress you are here. Please wait in the drawing room." Stoughton directed Kit to a room off the foyer.

Already Kit could see the changes made to the house. Doors off the foyer were open, and Kit could see that what once were private rooms were now classrooms. The drawing room was not at all conventional either. It looked more like a book room, an extension of the library. Books occupied every shelf and surface, and an array of different sofas were positioned at odd angles to allow private reading and conversation.

The house seemed quite quiet, so he assumed the students were out and about enjoying their weekend.

No sooner had Kit chosen one of the odd settees to sit down on, the door to the drawing room flung open. Kit spun around and there she was.

He froze as he looked on her for the first time in nine years. She was still so beautiful, just as he had remembered. Her skin was pale, like porcelain, and perhaps showed her maturity around the eyes a little, just as his now did. Her beautiful blue eyes were wide, but wise. They shone experience. She wore her lovely red hair down, as she always had, with a few pieces pinned back. It still had is natural wave and hung around her waist. She wore a sturdy, practical navy gown on her delicate figure, something fitting for a college founder. She looked like a grown woman now. Kit hoped that he had aged as well in her eyes and she had in his.

"Stoughton told me you were here and I couldn't quite believe my ears," Olivia remarked breathlessly after a long silence.

"Would you sit down with me?" Kit asked her. His voice was remarkably stead, not at all an accurate representation of how he was feeling on the inside.

Olivia nodded and tentatively walked over to the settee he was standing in front of. She sat down and smoothed out her skirt. Kit sat down beside her, though leaving a distance between them. Olivia showed the nerves Kit was feeling internally.

"What you have done here is incredible," he said softly.

She dared to look up at him, her vulnerability showing. "I am so glad you approve."

"You never needed my approval."

Olivia laughed lightly. "No, I didn't. But of anyone's opinion, yours is the one I value most."

"I kept up my end of the bargain, you know," Kit added.

Olivia furrowed her eyebrows. "What?"

"My education reform bill passed this week," he replied.

Olivia realised what he was talking about. "I read that in the newspaper. Compulsory schooling for boys to thirteen and girls to fifteen. You cannot know how happy I was to see you achieve such change."

"It took long enough," Kit joked and then took a deep breath. This light, nervous conversation was not what he was here to discuss. He had already failed at this once before.

But Olivia beat him to it. "I should have known you would have never made me become a political wife," she exclaimed suddenly. "I thought I needed to go it alone, but I should have known you would have supported whatever I decided to do, even if it involved leaving London." Olivia was turned to face him, her hand gripping the back of the sofa.

"Are you happy, Olivia? Have you achieved everything that you wanted?"

Olivia bit down on her bottom lip for a moment. "I have created something that I am so incredibly proud of. I have achieved goals that I never thought I could. I have goals now that I want to pursue. But I know I am not as happy in myself then when I was when I was working alongside you," she confessed.

Kit's heart seized in his chest. He was on edge as she continued.

"You knew my lofty ambition, to change the world. I somehow convinced myself that being married would get in my way. I know I was too young back then, Kit, but I was wrong to reject the idea entirely. I don't think I understood how good you were, Kit. I tell my girls to only accept a man if she can answer yes to these questions." Olivia took a breath. "Does he love me?"

"Yes," Kit replied.

Olivia paused, not realised that Kit had intended to respond. He watched as her blue eyes became glassy. She was trembling. Kit took the hand that had been gripping the sofa and he squeezed it comfortingly.

"Do you support me?" she continued, her voice shaking.

Kit looked into her eyes. "Yes."

"Do you listen to me?"

Always. "Yes."

"Do you believe in me?"

More than anyone. "Yes."

Olivia smiled as the tears began to fall from her eyes. "Do you advocate for me?"

Kit smiled. He would always advocate for her. "Yes."

Olivia used her free hand to wipe her face, smiling, laughing, as she cried. "How can you say these things after how I left?"

"I will not lie to you, Olivia. I can say that I have experienced a whole hoard of emotions and feelings, thoughts and opinions on the manner in which we left things. But what we need to know is that we were both young with big dreams and high ambitions and we did not get married. It is in the past. What happened made us who we are today. We are older, more mature, and ready, I hope, to take on this world together." Kit hoped what he was saying was making sense. He could hardly hear himself over the thunder in his chest.

Olivia beamed through her tears. "I am. I am ready now," she promised.

Elation filled Kit as he said, "I don't have a ring," comically.

Olivia laughed. "I noticed Lucy was wearing it."

Lucy still wore the ring Kit had given her for her eleventh birthday. She didn't know that it was meant to be Olivia's engagement ring. But it belonged to Lucy now. It was purchased by a different man for a different woman.

They would start afresh. "I don't want a wife," Kit said with conviction. "I want a partner. I am about to take a big step in my career, just as you are, and we shall help each other. There has never been anyone else for me. It was always you, Olivia," Kit said sincerely. "Will you marry me?"

Kit did not have a chance to be nervous about her answer. Olivia practically launched at him, landing on his lap as she pressed her lips to his eagerly. Kit reciprocated immediately, wrapping his arms around her tightly and holding her close.

Olivia kissed him repeatedly, moving away from his lips and kissing whatever part of his face she could find.

"Is that a yes?" Kit chuckled between kisses.

"Oh!" cried Olivia, pulling away and cupping his face. "Yes, yes, of course."

A joy like he hadn't felt in years filled Kit as he kissed her again.

There was much to talk about, much to work out, and surely conflicts to arise. They were both very determined people with big futures ahead of them. But they would handle it together. They were better together. They would make a happy life together.